The Art of

A PLAY

By Tina Howe

SAMUEL FRENCH, INC.

45 WEST 25TH STREET   NEW YORK 10010
7623 SUNSET BOULEVARD   HOLLYWOOD 90046
LONDON

NEW YORK SHAKESPEARE FESTIVAL
Joseph Papp, Producer
in association with
JOHN F. KENNEDY CENTER
FOR THE PERFORMING ARTS

presents

The Art of Dining

By **TINA HOWE**

Directed by **A. J. ANTOON**

Scenery by **DAVID JENKINS**
Costumes by **HILARY ROSENFELD**
Lighting by **IAN CALDERON**
Hair and Make-up by **J. ROY HELLAND**

with

KATHY BATES
SUZANNE COLLINS
ROBERT GERRINGER
GEORGE GUIDALL
JANE HOFFMAN
JACKLYN MADDUX
RON RIFKIN
MARGARET WHITTON
DIANNE WIEST

JOHN F. KENNEDY CENTER FOR THE PERFORMING ARTS
Roger L. Stevens, Producer

CAST

(In Order of Speaking)

ELLEN	*Suzanne Collins*
CAL	*Ron Rifkin*
HANNAH GALT	*Jane Hoffman*
PAUL GALT	*Robert Gerringer*
ELIZABETH BARROW COLT	*Dianne Wiest*
HERRICK SIMMONS	*Kathy Bates*
NESSA VOX	*Margaret Whitton*
TONY STASSIO	*Jacklyn Maddux*
DAVID OSSLOW	*George Guidall*

TIME: The present. Early evening.

PLACE: The Golden Carrousel Restaurant, New Jersey.

5

CHARACTERS

(In order of appearance)

ELLEN—*co-owner and chef extraordinaire of The Golden Carrousel, mid 30's.*

CAL—*co-owner and supple head waiter of The Golden Carrousel, Ellen's husband, mid 30's.*

HANNAH GALT—*beautifully dressed and hungry, mid 40's.*

PAUL GALT—*beautifully dressed and hungrier, mid 40's.*

ELIZABETH BARROW COLT—*exceedingly shy and near-sighted. A writer, in her early 30's, afraid of food.*

HERRICK SIMMONS—*enthusiastic and a good eater, early 30's.*

NESSA VOX—*easily upset and a more neurotic eater, early 30's.*

TONY STASSIO—*perpetually on a diet and miserable, early 30's.*

DAVID OSSLOW—*the head of his own publishing company, successful, at ease, son and husband of good cooks, mid 50's and in top shape.*

The Art of Dining

ACT ONE

SCENE 1

The ground floor of a 19th century townhouse on the New Jersey shore which has been converted into a restaurant, The Golden Carrousel. It's a wonderfully elegant little place with a high tin ceiling, arched windows, and masses of hanging plants. A pair of restored carrousel horses with flashing gold manes or hooves prance in a corner. A surreal nostalgia suffuses the room. Things are on the verge of lifting off the ground or disappearing entirely. Nothing is quite what it seems. Embedded within, behind, or to one side of this magical dining area is a full working kitchen. Though many of its features are old — sink, lighting fixtures, ornate moulding, for example — it's equipped with all the most up to date appliances... It's late November, unusually cold, and a month after the restaurant's grand opening. Four tables are set for dinner, and the fragrance of the evening's offerings fills the air.

ELLEN *and* CAL *are sitting at one of the tables about to sample two different desserts. They should be mistaken for customers.*

ELLEN. (*Tense with expectancy, dips her spoon into her glass of Floating Island, tastes it and holds her breath.*)

CAL. (*Stabs his spoon into his dish of Pears and*

7

Cointreau with Frozen Cream and croons with delight.)

ELLEN. (*Savors her mouthful and exhales with relief.*)

CAL. (*Very rapidly takes another taste, a long sigh.*)

ELLEN. (*Takes a cautious second taste and makes a humming sound.*)

CAL. (*Takes three rapid fire tastes, making little whimpering sounds after each one.*)

ELLEN. (*Licks her lips and pauses.*)

CAL. (*Scraping his spoon against the sides of his dish with fervor, takes a heaping mouthful and groans with pleasure.*)

ELLEN. (*Takes another apprehensive taste. Yes, it's excellent, she purrs.*)

CAL. (*Overcome, drops his head in his hands.*)

ELLEN. (*Puts her spoon down and nods her head yes. Silence. Shoves her dessert over to* CAL *to try. He dips his spoon in, takes a slow loving taste. It's even better than his! He moans helplessly and pushes his dessert over to her.* ELLEN *takes a swift taste of the pears, making little lip smacking noises.*)

CAL. (*Takes a huge spoonful of Floating Island and is mute.*)

(*A silence.*)

ELLEN. (*Exhales with pleasure. Takes another taste, inhales, stares into space, puts her spoon down, clicks her tongue, exhilerated.*)

CAL. (*Takes a smaller taste, then makes a low sob and takes five very fast spoonfuls grunting during each one.*)

(*A silence.*)

ELLEN. (*Reaches across the table and takes back her*

Floating Island and returns the pears to CAL. *She scrapes the sides of her glass.*)

CAL. (*Fiercely attacks what's left of his pears.*)

(*They finish, breathing heavily.*)

CAL. (*Weakly.*) Pears . . .
ELLEN. (*Undone.*) Meringues . . .
CAL. Cointreau . . .
ELLEN. Vanilla . . .
CAL. Heavy cream . . .
ELLEN. Caramel . . .
CAL. Chilled . . .
ELLEN. Poached . . .
CAL. Cool . . .
ELLEN. Quivering . . .
CAL. . . . to perfection!
ELLEN. In English Cream!
CAL. Pure sin!
ELLEN. Real joy.
CAL. A person could die . . .
ELLEN. Which did you like better?
CAL. What a way to go!
ELLEN. The pears . . .
CAL. Christ!
ELLEN. . . . or the Floating Island?
CAL. (*Frantically scrapes at his dish, nothing is left.*)
ELLEN. I preferred the pears, didn't you?
CAL. (*Reaching for her dish.*) Do you have any left?
ELLEN. They're more challenging. (*She picks up* CAL's *empty dish and rises. Wipes invisible crumbs from the table, straightens the table cloth as.*)
CAL. (*Scrapes his spoon in* ELLEN's *dish for the last bits of Floating Island then plunges his finger in and starts scraping the sides.*)
ELLEN. (*Going into the kitchen. She puts* CAL's *dish in*

the sink and starts stirring the soup on the stove as.)

CAL. (*Scraping the sides of his dish with alternate fingers and sucking them clean, rises and follows* ELLEN *into the kitchen. He looks around, finds the saucepan of warm Floating Island and pours more into his empty dish, gets a new spoon and takes slow loving mouthfuls as he watches* ELLEN *work on her soup.)*

(These are the various works in progress:
Belgian Oxtail Soup
Billi Bi on a low flame
Several ducks browning in a heavy frying pan
Veal
Wild rice

Set aside on the counters are the beginnings of:
The stuffing for the veal
The shrimp mousse for the bass
A huge tossed salad
A saucepan full of Floating Island

Hidden in the refrigerator are:
The Pears in Cointreau with Frozen Cream
The uncooked bass
Basic ingredients for the sauces, Hollandaise and Velouté.
Celery
A bowl of grapes for the duck

ELLEN. (*Stirring and tasting her soup.*) They were firm enough, weren't they?

CAL. (*Involved with his Floating Island.*) Oh . . . so smooth!

ELLEN. Nothing is worse than limp pears!

CAL. . . . so light . . .

ELLEN. What time is it?

CAL. . . . perfect!

ELLEN. They were all right, weren't they?

CAL. (*Referring to the Floating Island.*) You added something.

ELLEN. (*Referring to the pears.*) I added something.

CAL. What is it? I can't tell.

ELLEN. A touch of . . . ginger.

CAL. (*Smacking his lips.*) It tastes more like . . . cinnamon . . .

ELLEN. . . . and a hint of almond.

CAL. No wait, I've got it . . .

ELLEN. Did you notice?

CAL. NUTMEG!

ELLEN. (*Tasting the soup.*) I'll bet you didn't even notice the almond.

CAL. It's nutmeg.

ELLEN. The ginger flavor is much stronger.

CAL. It's wonderful.

ELLEN. How much time do we have?

CAL. Really delicious.

ELLEN. (*Offering him a taste of soup.*) What do you think? I don't know, the bouquet's a little weak . . .

CAL. (*Referring to the Floating Island.*) You should make it more often, everyone loves it.

ELLEN. It needs more thyme for one thing.

CAL. (*Gobbling up the rest of the Floating Island.*) I can't stop eating this Floating Island! I don't know what you do to your desserts, this is irresistible!

ELLEN. (*Holding out a spoonful of soup.*) I need you to taste. How is it?

CAL. It tastes like Floating Island.

ELLEN. Come on Cal, they'll be here soon. Try again.

CAL. Oh, I forgot to tell you, Table Four cancelled because of the bad weather.

ELLEN. They'll come back . . . (*Holding out a fresh taste of soup.*) Now tell me; how is it?

CAL. (*Takes his time, savors it.*) Good.

ELLEN. *Good?* Is that all?

CAL. (*Helps himself to another spoonful.*) Very good.

ELLEN. Damn! . . . (*She has another taste.*) The bouquet's still weak . . .

CAL. (*Strides over to her with his spoon, starts dipping it into the soup and slurping.*)

ELLEN. (*Tastes in a much more exacting way.*) Wait a minute!

CAL. VERY GOOD!

ELLEN. I FORGOT THE WATERCRESS!

CAL. . . . and this is without the added touches of smoked ham and Madeira.

ELLEN. (*Laughing, gets the watercress from the refrigerator.*) I forgot the watercress.

CAL. It's perfect, it doesn't need watercress!

ELLEN. What do you mean, it doesn't need watercress?

CAL. It's delicious without watercress.

ELLEN. It's incomplete without watercress! (*She adds some.*)

CAL. Watercress is over rated.

ELLEN. Watercress is *essential!*

CAL. Watercress is a pain in the ass!

ELLEN. Watercress is one of the staples of French and Chinese cuisine!

CAL. It's over rated.

ELLEN. It's piquant . . .

CAL. It's soggy . . .

ELLEN. It's refreshing . . .

CAL. It's overpriced . . .

(*The telephone rings. There are two phones in the kitchen. Depending on where he's standing,* CAL *alternates between them.*)

ELLEN. Oh God! (*She works faster on her soup.*)

CAL. I've got it! (*On the phone.*) Good evening, The Golden Carrousel, may I help you?

ELLEN. God, God, God!

CAL. Reservations for two this Friday night at eight? . . . Hold on a sec, let me check our calendar. (*To* ELLEN.) Reservations for two this Friday at eight.

ELLEN. We're filled for the rest of the week!

CAL. (*Back on the phone, eyeing the calendar.*) Yes, I see a space.

ELLEN. We're filled!

CAL. Could I have your name, please? . . . I'm sorry, would you mind spelling that for me?

ELLEN. (*In an urgent whisper.*) I'm making apricot brandy souffles on Friday!

CAL. K.A.S.T.F.S.

ELLEN. I have to prepare a fresh apricot puree for each one.

CAL. (*Slower.*) K.A.S.T.O.F.S.K. . . . WHAT?

ELLEN. It makes all the difference.

CAL. O.F.S.K.*Y*!

ELLEN. That way, the full apricot aroma is retained until the very last.

CAL. *Kas*tofsky.

ELLEN. If you make the puree beforehand and let it sit until the souffle is ready to pour then . . .

CAL. Oh, Kas*tof*sky, I'm sorry!

ELLEN. Apricot is very delicate.

CAL. (*Pleased.*) KasTOFsky!

ELLEN. Much more so than lemon or orange, a lemon souffle . . .

CAL. Yes, Kas*tof*sky. I've got it now!

ELLEN. Or even a strawberry souffle would be . . .

CAL. Well, thank you for calling, Mr. Kastofsky. We'll see you on Friday night then at 8. Good-bye. (*He hangs up. To* ELLEN, *radiant.*) WHAT DID I TELL YOU?

ELLEN. Apricot is tricky.

CAL. (*Adding the Kastofskys to their calendar which is already black with reservations.*) The word is spreading! We've only been open four weeks and we're already booked into next month!

ELLEN. I can't cook for more than two sittings a night.

CAL. They're breaking down the doors . . .

ELLEN. We've been over this before.

CAL. Jamming the phones . . .

ELLEN. If you rush me, the food will suffer.

CAL. (*Goes to the second pot of soup on the stove, the Billi Bi, and helps himself to a huge spoonful. He burns his tongue and yowls in pain jumping up and down.*)

ELLEN. (*Rushing over to him.*) What happened?

CAL. (*Keeps yowling, his tongue hanging out.*)

ELLEN. I can't understand you . . .

CAL. (*Completely garbled since his tongue is out.*) I burned my tongue!

ELLEN. Oh baby!

CAL. (*Jumping up and down.*) Get me the boric acid!

(*The telephone starts to ring.*)

ELLEN. (*Rushes to the refrigerator.*) I'm getting the butter! (*She returns with a stick of butter.*)

CAL. (*Garbled.*) Not butter, boric acid!

ELLEN. What?

CAL. (*Garbled.*) I SAID, *BORIC ACID!*

ELLEN. Hold still, this will numb the pain . . .

CAL. Answer the phone!

ELLEN. What?

CAL. (*Waving towards the ringing phone.*) The phone, the phone, the phone!

ELLEN. Hold still, or I can't get it on.

CAL. (*Garbled.*) Will you answer the goddamned phone???!

ELLEN. I know it hurts, honey, just hang on one minute! (*She starts smearing butter on his flapping tongue.*)

CAL. (*More garbled than ever.*) I DON'T WANT BUTTER! I WANT BORIC ACID. BORIC ACID!

ELLEN. (*Imitates the way he says it to try and understand him.*) Boric acid?

CAL. Will you please answer the phone before they hang up.

ELLEN. (*Says Boric Acid as before, completely confused.*) Boric acid??

CAL. (*Lunges for the phone, tongue still out and incomprehensible.*) Good evening, The Golden Carrousel, may I help you?

ELLEN. (*Takes the phone from him.*) Oh! The telephone!

CAL. (*Puts his tongue back in his mouth, as clear as day.*) The telephone.

ELLEN. Well, why didn't you say so? (*Into the phone.*) Good evening, The Golden Carrousel, could you hold on for just a moment please? (*She puts the receiver aside. To* CAL.) Now, what is it that you want?

CAL. (*His tongue in his mouth, clearly.*) Boric acid.

ELLEN. (*Amazed.*) Ohhhh! Boric acid! You mean, *Baking Soda!*

CAL. (*Sticks out his tongue and says it all queer again.*)

ELLEN. (*Copies him. Keeping her tongue out,*

garbled.) Coming right up. (*She gets it from a cupboard.*)

CAL. (*His tongue out.*) I think I burned off all the skin.

ELLEN. (*Laughing, imitates him again.*) I think I burned off all the skin!

CAL. (*His tongue back in, clear.*) I burned off all the skin.

ELLEN. (*Gently fingering his tongue.*) No you didn't. It's just a bit red. Now hold still so I can get this butter off.

CAL. (*Garbled again.*) At least you could have used sweet butter!

ELLEN. (*Tongue out, imitates what he said.*)

CAL. (*Tongue back in.*) Sweet butter.

ELLEN. Sweet butter! (*Puts some baking soda on his tongue.*) How does that feel?

CAL. It hurts.

ELLEN. I'm sorry. Did you enjoy the soup at least?

CAL. I couldn't taste it.

ELLEN. I haven't added the egg yolks yet.

CAL. (*In pain.*) Son of a bitch.

ELLEN. They make all the difference . . .

CAL. (*Touching his tongue.*) I burned off all my damned taste buds!

ELLEN. (*Gently blowing on his tongue.*) No you didn't, it's just red.

CAL. That feels good.

ELLEN. (*Keeps blowing on it.*) Poor baby.

CAL. They're so fragile.

ELLEN. What are?

CAL. Taste buds.

ELLEN. That's because they're nerves.

CAL. . . . Millions of tiny fragile pink dots. They have roots, you know. Long roots that extend all the way through your tongue . . . they're like the fingers on a hand . . . long sensitive fingers, touching and feeling . . . and now I've burned them all off . . . OH JESUS, THE TELEPHONE! (*He rushes to the telephone.*) Hello? Are you still there? Hello? Hello? (*He slams the receiver down.*) They hung up! (ELLEN *laughs.*) It's not funny.

ELLEN. They'll call back.

CAL. How do you know? (*He goes to the refrigerator and starts looking for something to eat.*)

ELLEN. We've got to hurry!

CAL. (*Making a racket moving things about.*) We might have lost a customer just now.

ELLEN. It's getting late.

CAL. They probably won't call back.

ELLEN. (*Holding out a spoonful of soup to him.*) Come on, open.

CAL. (*Pulls out a bowl of green grapes set aside to garnish the duckling in wine, fitfully starts eating them.*) Ellen, we've borrowed $75,000 to open this place, and if we don't come up with 20,000 next month, the whole thing will go under. Good-bye. Gone. We can't afford to lose any phone calls.

ELLEN. (*The spoon still extended.*) Please.

CAL. (*Woolfing down the grapes.*) We've got to clear $900 a night!

ELLEN. . . . taste!

CAL. . . . and if we don't serve a minimum of 36 customers a night . . .

ELLEN. No!

CAL. . . . at approximately $35 each . . .

ELLEN. Cal!

CAL. We won't clear that $900!

ELLEN. Please . . .

CAL. We're so close!

ELLEN. (*Offers him a fresh spoonful, blows on it.*) Taste . . .

CAL. (*Eating the grapes with more relish.*) We could really do it!

ELLEN. Do you like it?

CAL. Serve outstanding food *and* make money at the same time!

ELLEN. Is it all right?

(*The telephone rings.*)

CAL. (*Pushes past her and grabs the phone.*) There they are!

ELLEN. (*Working on her soup.*) I'm falling behind.

CAL. (*On the phone while popping grapes in his mouth.*) Good evening, The Golden Carrousel. Did you just call us? (*To* ELLEN.) *It's them!* (*On the phone.*) I'm sorry, we had a slight . . . may I help you? Three for next Tuesday? Let me check our calendar.

ELLEN. We're filled.

CAL. (*Looking at the calendar.*) What time was that again? 9 o'clock? Just one moment, please.

ELLEN. We're filled for the entire week. Hey, don't eat all those grapes. I need them for the Duckling in Wine with Green Grapes!

CAL. Yes, I see a space. We could fit you in at nine.

ELLEN. I'm never going to make it.

CAL. Your name, please?

ELLEN. Never!

CAL. Canelli? . . . Thank you very much for calling, Mr. Canelli.

CAL. We'll be expecting you next Tuesday at nine, then.

ELLEN. Cal, we're booked!

CAL. Your friends said it was the best restaurant in the United States? (*To* ELLEN.) . . . the best restaurant in the United States! (*Back on the phone.*) And they've eaten everywhere? (*To* ELLEN.) They've eaten *everywhere!*

ELLEN. I haven't even started the celery or begun the sauce velouté. . . .

CAL. (*On the phone.*) You've already sent five couples here . . . ? (*To* ELLEN.) *Five* couples!

ELLEN. (*Snapping off the tops of the celery.*) Don't panic.

CAL. They loved it!

ELLEN. You see, they loved it!

CAL. (*On the phone.*) Thank you very much for your kind words. I hope we'll be able to live up to them for you next Tuesday. Goodbye. (*He hangs up, pops more grapes in his mouth.*) They can't get enough!

ELLEN. (*Feeling overwhelmed.*) Oh boy!

CAL. They're coming back! A second time, a third time!

ELLEN. Oh boy, oh boy!

CAL. They're telling their friends!

ELLEN. (*Frantically washing, scraping, and cutting the celery.*) Oh boy oh boy oh boy *oh boy!*

CAL. And those friends are telling other friends!

ELLEN. (*Faster and faster.*) OH BOY OH BOY OH BOY!

CAL. (*Lunges back into the bowl of grapes.*) This is just the beginning!

ELLEN. (*Makes a small strangled sound.*)

CAL. We can't lose!

ELLEN. (*Another sound.*)

CAL. The chance of a lifetime!

(*The doorbell rings.*)

ELLEN. (*Whispered.*) They're here! CAL. (*Whispered.*) The door!

ELLEN. (*Grabs an onion, starts chopping it.*) Help!

CAL. Relax! (*He reaches for a black bow tie and starts putting it on.*)

ELLEN. They're here.

CAL. (*Sings his favorite show tune under his breath.*)

ELLEN. I'm not ready. . . . no where *near* ready! There's still the wine sauce for the duck and the hollandaise, not to mention the shrimp mousse for the bass . . .

CAL. (*Sings on, preening.*)

ELLEN. Oh well, it's just par for the course, right? RIGHT???! (*Notices the empty bowl.*) Where did all the Floating Island go?

(*The doorbell rings again.*)

CAL. Just a minute . . .

ELLEN. You ate all the Floating Island!

CAL. (*Still singing, bolts upstairs to get his tuxedo jacket.*)

ELLEN. (*Gazing into the empty bowl.*) He ate all the Floating Island. Our first customers of the evening have arrived . . . and he's eaten half the desserts . . .

CAL. (*Bounds back into the kitchen, splendid in his tuxedo. He salutes* ELLEN.) We're off! (*Out the door.*) Coming . . .

ELLEN. (*Goes to the sink, angrily turns on the faucet to wash the celery.*) I don't believe this! (*The lights fade on her and rise on* CAL *advancing to the front door.*)

SCENE 2

CAL *is a changed person in his tuxedo jacket. He glitters with charm, elegance, and the desire to please. He opens the door.*

PAUL and HANNAH GALT. (*Are literally blown in. They're in their middle 40's and are suptuously dressed: he in a hand tailored suit under a cashmere coat, she in a floating crepe dress under a mink coat.*)

CAL. (*Bowing slightly.*) Good evening. The Galt party? Won't you come in?

HANNAH. (*Shivering so violently she totters.*) Oooooooooh, it's soooooooooo cold!

PAUL. (*Slapping his gloved hands together.*) That wind is . . .

HANNAH. I've never been so . . .

PAUL. WICKED!

CAL. (*Reaching for* HANNAH's *coat.*) May I?

HANNAH. Cold!

PAUL. It's got to be 40 below out there!

CAL. (*Reaching for* PAUL's *coat.*) Sir?

HANNAH. . . . unbearable!

PAUL. And with the wind chill factor, it's more like 60 below.

HANNAH. . . . and only *November!*

CAL. They say the worst is yet to come.

HANNAH. (*Hands over her ears.*) Don't . . .

PAUL. (*To* CAL.) Yes, I heard that too. Arctic storms are due down from Canada sometime in mid January . . .

CAL. (*To* PAUL.) In February we're supposed to have the worst blizzard this country has ever seen! The National Guard's being prepared for this one . . .

HANNAH. (*Looking around the room.*) Oh Paul, look! It's charming!

CAL. Please, won't you follow me to your table? We'll warm you up in no time? (*He pulls out the chair for* HANNAH.) Madame?

HANNAH. (*Is enthralled with one of the horses.*) Ooooooh, merry-go-round horses!

PAUL. (*Unwittingly sits down in the chair meant for* HANNAH.)

CAL. *Monsieur!*

HANNAH. I love them!

PAUL. (*To* CAL, *sitting down*.) Thank you.

HANNAH. I WANT THEM!

PAUL. I haven't felt wind like that since . . .

HANNAH. Aren't they wonderful?

CAL. Could I warm you up with something from the bar?

PAUL. (*Sighs, looking around*.) This is very nice.

CAL. . . . a cocktail?

PAUL. Oh look, Hannah. They have your merry-go-round horses!

HANNAH. They're almost impossible to find these days.

CAL. Some sherry?

PAUL. Those are old!

HANNAH. Aren't they wonderful? I wonder where they got them?

CAL. (*To* HANNAH.) Would you care for something from the bar?

HANNAH. I'll bet you've gotten plenty of offers for those . . .

PAUL. I don't know about you, but I am starved!

HANNAH. (*To* CAL.) A word of advice: Don't sell them!

CAL. A glass of white wine . . . ?

PAUL. I could eat a horse!

HANNAH. . . . no matter what they offer you!

PAUL. I need a drink!

CAL. Yes sir?

HANNAH. (*To* CAL.) Every year, they triple in value!

CAL. Give me a double scotch, straight up.

CAL. Very good, and you Madame?

HANNAH. (*Comes to the table and sits down.*) *You hang on to them!*

PAUL. I don't know why I should be so hungry, I had a perfectly good lunch!

HANNAH. (*To* PAUL, *under her breath.*) God, I'd love to get my hands on those!

CAL. And for you, Madame?

PAUL. Tartar steak and salad . . .

HANNAH. Let's see, I guess I'll have a Vodka Gimlet.

CAL. Thank you. (*He retires to the bar area to mix their drinks.*)

PAUL. I even had a pastry for dessert.

HANNAH. I'm hungry.

PAUL. A plum tart . . .

HANNAH. I only had a small omelette for lunch.

PAUL. . . . with an apricot glaze.

HANNAH. Mushroom . . .

PAUL. It was . . . incredible!

HANNAH. . . . with a hint of dill.

PAUL. Melt . . . in . . . your . . . mouth.

HANNAH. I behaved myself and skipped dessert.

PAUL. I almost ordered a second.

HANNAH. What did you have for lunch today?

PAUL. *Almost* . . .

HANNAH. I hardly had anything . . .

PAUL. You should have seen the plum tart I had for dessert . . .

HANNAH. Just an omelette.

PAUL. The pastry shell alone . . .

HANNAH. I thought of having a muffin with it . . .

PAUL. . . . was unbelievable!

HANNAH. Only a half, of course . . .

PAUL. It could have been served on its own.

HANNAH. But I didn't.

PAUL. I almost broke down and had a second.

HANNAH. Paul!

PAUL. I know, I know!

HANNAH. You shouldn't even *think* of having a second dessert!

PAUL. Well, did I have it? Did I?

HANNAH. I don't know. How would I know?

PAUL. I JUST SAID THAT I DIDN'T. JESUS! (*A silence.*)

HANNAH. I only had an omelette . . . (*A silence.*)

PAUL. I didn't have a second dessert, all right???!

HANNAH. . . . a small mushroom omelette . . .

PAUL. All right????

HANNAH. (*Patting her stomach.*) Uuuuh, it was so filling! (*A silence.*)

PAUL. (*Depressed, sighs.*)

HANNAH. It's amazing how filling a small mushroom omelette is . . . but then again mushrooms are very . . . starchy . . . (*A silence.*)

CAL. (*Returns from the bar, puts down* HANNAH's *drink with a flourish.*) A Vodka Gimlet for Madame!

HANNAH. Thank you very much.

CAL. (*Sensing the tension between them, sets down* PAUL's *drink with even more flair.*) And a double scotch for you, Sir. I hope you enjoy it.

HANNAH. (*Leans back, takes a long sip of her drink, sighs.*)

PAUL. (*Mutters and takes a gulp.*)

CAL. Would you be interested in seeing the menu now, or would you rather wait?

PAUL. Yes, now please.   HANNAH. Oh, let's wait!

CAL. (*More and more flashy in his gestures.*) Very good, I'll bring them right over. (*He fetches them and hands one to* HANNAH.) Madame?

HANNAH. Now, what was it that Ken and Diva said was so good?

CAL. (*Handing one to* PAUL.) Monsier?

HANNAH. Sole Veronique?

PAUL. (*Under his breath.*) You know I'd never have two desserts for lunch on a day we were going out for dinner!

HANNAH. . . . or was it Sole Meuniere?

PAUL. I'm not that stupid!

HANNAH. No wait, I think it was Sole Florentine!

PAUL. . . . and in case you've forgotten, I jogged three miles after I got home from the office.

HANNAH. I'VE GOT IT! IT WAS SOLE BONNE FEMME!

PAUL. In fact, it was closer to four and a half.

HANNAH. Ken had Poulet Farci . . . and Diva had Sole Bonne Femme!

PAUL. I've never been in such good shape!

HANNAH. Or was it the other way around?

PAUL. (*Punching his stomach.*) See that? Hard as a rock!

HANNAH. Ken had the Sole Bonne Femme, and Diva had the Poulet Farci!

PAUL. Go on, hit me in the stomach, I won't even feel it!

HANNAH. No, wait a minute . . .

PAUL. (*Thrusting out his stomach.*) Come on!

HANNAH. Diva had Poulet Bonne Femme . . .

PAUL. Hit me!

HANNAH. . . . and Ken had Sole Farci!

PAUL. (*Slugs himself.*) See, I didn't feel a thing!

HANNAH. No, that can't be right. There's no such dish as Sole Farci.

PAUL. I'll do it harder. (*He does.*) Nothing . . . !

HANNAH. Anyway, both of them said it was the most delicious Sole Bonne Femme they'd ever had!

PAUL. (*Really socks himself.*) See that? Didn't even feel it. (*A silence.*) Want me to do it again? (*He repeatedly socks himself in the stomach. A silence. Then cheerful.*) What was it that Ken and Diva said was so good?

HANNAH. I'm in the mood for veal.

PAUL. Sole Almondine?

HANNAH. You know how on some days you wake up with a craving for something?

CAL. (*Hovering nearby.*) We change our menus every day.

PAUL. Oh?

HANNAH. Friends of ours had your Sole Bonne Femme last week. They said it was out of this world!

CAL. Yes, my wife is a remarkable cook.

HANNAH. Oh, it's your wife who's the chef. I didn't know that.

PAUL. Remember that Chicken Bonne Femme we had at the Pavillion years ago?

HANNAH. It's very rare to come across a woman who's a paid chef.

PAUL. Remember the sauce . . . ?

HANNAH. There are only a handful in this country.

PAUL. . . . with white wine and truffles . . .

CAL. Julia Child . . .

HANNAH. Dionne Lucas.

CAL. She's been dead for several years.

HANNAH. She died? I didn't know that!

PAUL. . . . salt pork and meat glaze . . .

CAL. There aren't many.

PAUL. . . . and remember the baby potatoes served with it?

HANNAH. (*To* CAL.) Do you cook too?

CAL. No, I'm afraid I just eat.

HANNAH. We both cook.

CAL. How nice!

HANNAH. (*Nodding towards* PAUL.) He's very good.

PAUL. (*Fingering his menu.*) Well, shall we begin?

CAL. I'm sure.

HANNAH. He does much better soups than me.

CAL. Soups are tricky.

PAUL. (*Holding up his menu.*) Are you ready?

HANNAH. You should taste his gazpacho!

CAL. I love gazpacho!

HANNAH. Well you should taste his . . . ! (*She purrs, remembering the taste.*)

PAUL. (*Holding out her menu for her.*) Hannah!

HANNAH. . . . out . . . of . . . this . . . world!

PAUL. Are you ready?

HANNAH. (*Sighs again.*)

PAUL. I'm opening mine . . . (*He looks at her and waits.*)

CAL. If I can assist you in any way, just . . .

PAUL. Hannah, I'm hungry!

CAL. (*Goes to the rear of the room and flicks on the opening movement of J.S. Bach's Sonata No. 3 in E major for violin and harpsichord. The opening measures sound before the* GALTS *begin.*)

PAUL. (*Flicks open his menu with a meaningful look.*)

HANNAH. (*Follows suit.*)

PAUL. (*Glances down the length of it, a tremulous sigh.*)

HANNAH. (*Also glances but in tense silence.*)

PAUL. (*Inhales, takes a deep breath.*)

HANNAH. (*Pushes a strand of hair up off her forehead.*)

PAUL. (*Exhales.*)

HANNAH. (*Tosses her head in bewilderment.*)

PAUL. (*Another sigh, louder.*)

(*Silence.*)

HANNAH. (*Overcome, shuts her menu and puts it face down on the table.*)

PAUL. (*Gently picks it up and hands it back to her, smiling.*)

HANNAH. (*Scans it again. It's such a feast of choices, she can't decide. She moans.*)

PAUL. (*Pushes back in his chair, eyeing the menu, narrows his eyes, inhales.*)

HANNAH. Oh Paul!

PAUL. (*Still looking at his menu covers her hand with his.*)

HANNAH. Its . . .

PAUL. Sssssssh!

HANNAH. (*Makes a helpless little sound.*)

PAUL. I know. I know.

HANNAH. Help me.

PAUL. Sweetheart!

HANNAH. Oh Paul!

PAUL. Take your time . . .

HANNAH. I . . .

PAUL. There's no rush . . .

HANNAH. I'm so . . .

PAUL. Relax.

HANNAH. (*With a sob.*) I can't!

PAUL. Of course you can!

HANNAH. (*Her head in her hands.*) I'm scared.

PAUL. (*Lifting her head up, cupping it in his hands.*) Trust me.

CAL. (*Turns up the volume of the music.*)

PAUL. (*Under his breath, to* CAL.) Not so loud.

CAL. Sorry! (*Lowers the volume.*)

PAUL. (*Leans close to* HANNAH *and points to something on her menu.*) To start . . .

HANNAH. (*Melting.*) Oh Paul . . . !

PAUL. (*Points to something else.*)

HANNAH. (*A low sexy giggle.*)

PAUL. (*Points again.*) And maybe . . .

HANNAH. (*Kisses him lightly and coos.*)

PAUL. (*Pointing to something else.*) Or, how about . . . ?

HANNAH. (*Goes off into a shower of giggles.*)

PAUL. (*Pointing.*) With a side order of . . .

HANNAH. (*Horrified, closes her menu on his hand.*) Paul!

PAUL. (*Reaches over and kisses her.*) Forgive me! (*A silence.*)

HANNAH. (*Suddenly aggressive, leans over him until she's almost in his lap. She points.*) OK . . . How about . . . ?

PAUL. (*Shocked.*) Hannah?

HANNAH. (*Pointing elsewhere.*) Plus some . . . (*They both go off into gales.*)

CAL. (*Watches them with amusement and laughs to himself.*)

PAUL. (*Out of breath.*) Stop it!

HANNAH. (*Points again.*) *And* . . .

PAUL. (*Reaches over and kisses her.*) Darling! You're being obscene and you know it!

HANNAH. (*Laughing, points again.*) And . . . for dessert!

PAUL. (*Noticing that* CAL *is watching them.*) People are staring . . .

CAL. (*Quickly looks the other way as.*)

HANNAH. (*Shoots him a dirty look.*)

(*The doorbell rings.*)

CAL. (*Saved, heads for the door.*)

(*The lights fade on the* GALTS. *The music stops.*)

SCENE 3

CAL. (*Opens the door.*) Yes?

ELIZABETH BARROW COLT. (*Staggers in. She's terribly shy and nervous and very nearsighted. A writer, in her early 30's, she's almost paralyzed with awkwardness. When she speaks she's completely inaudible.*)

CAL. Good evening, you're with the un . . . which party?

ELIZABETH BARROW COLT. (*Inaudible.*) I'm meeting David Osslow.

CAL. Pardon me?

ELIZABETH BARROW COLT. (*Inaudible.*) Mr. Osslow.

CAL. (*Straining to hear.*) I'm sorry . . .

ELIZABETH BARROW COLT. (*In a terrified whisper, looks around the room.*) David Osslow.

CAL. (*Looking at his reservations list.*) Ah yes, David Osslow!

ELIZABETH BARROW COLT. (*Cringes.*)

CAL. He hasn't come yet. May I take your coat and show you to your table?

ELIZABETH BARROW COLT. (*Panic-stricken.*) I'm early?

CAL. I beg your pardon?

ELIZABETH BARROW COLT. Oh dear.

CAL. Let me take your coat and I'll show you to your table.

ELIZABETH BARROW COLT. (*Clutches her coat around her and stands rooted to the spot.*)

CAL. Wouldn't you like me to show you to your table? I'm sure Mr. Osslow will be here any minute.

ELIZABETH BARROW COLT. (*Looks around the room furtively, opens her pocketbook, and head lowered, takes out a comb and starts combing her hair. As she does, several things fall out of her pocketbook. She dives for them, bumping into CAL as he tries to help her retrieve them.*)

CAL. I'm sorry. Excuse me, I was just trying to . . . I'm sorry . . . wanted to help you get that . . . here's your toothbrush.

ELIZABETH BARROW COLT. Oh dear, I dropped my . . . I'm sorry, I didn't mean to . . . my lipstick and diary . . . oh dear!

CAL. (*Hands her a few things.*) Here, I hope I didn't . . .

ELIZABETH BARROW COLT. (*Very softly.*) I'm not wearing my glasses.

CAL. (*Jovial.*) It sure is cold out there!

ELIZABETH BARROW COLT. (*Dumping everything back into her pocketbook.*) I can't see very well . . .

CAL. (*Gently.*) May I take your coat?

ELIZABETH BARROW COLT. (*With a sudden wild giggle.*) I can't see anything at all! (*She sneaks her glasses out of her pocketbook and quickly holds them up to her eyes to get her bearings.*) OH, LOOK AT THOSE MERRY-GO-ROUND HORSES! GRACIOUS! (*She bumps into the serving cart which careens towards* HANNAH *who screams.*)

CAL. (*To the* GALTS.) I'm terribly sorry, I'll have her seated in just one moment . . .

ELIZABETH BARROW COLT. (*Opens her pocketbook again and head lowered, sneaks on a smear of bright lipstick.*)

CAL. I heard it's 30 below with the wind chill factor.

ELIZABETH BARROW COLT. (*Drops the lipstick back in her bag, reaches for her comb and combs her hair again.*) I look a mess.

CAL. And next year, if you can believe it, we're supposed to get hit even harder!

ELIZABETH BARROW COLT. (*Takes out her glasses again, puts them on for a second, lowers her head, and makes several strange low sobs.*)

CAL. (*Touching her.*) Could I take your coat for you?

ELIZABETH BARROW COLT. (*Her wild giggle again.*) OH . . . MY COAT!!! (*She fumbles with the buttons.*)

CAL. It's all right, take your time. (*Pause.*) We're supposed to get some relief over the weekend.

ELIZABETH BARROW COLT. (*As she struggles with her coat buttons, drops her bag again and everything spills out.*) Oh dear.

CAL. Here, I'll get it . . . (*He dives for the floor and scoops it all back into her bag which he finally hands to her.*) Here you go.

ELIZABETH BARROW COLT. (*Barely audible.*) I can't see very well.

CAL. I beg your pardon?

ELIZABETH BARROW COLT. I can't see very well.

CAL. (*Helping her off with her coat which becomes a great muddle as she can't get her arms out of the sleeves properly.*) Here, let me help you.

ELIZABETH BARROW COLT. (*Struggling between CAL and the coat.*) I'M AS BLIND AS A BAT!

CAL. (*Gets the coat off, sighs.*) Please . . . follow me. (*And he leads her to her table, pulling her chair way way out to give her plenty of leeway.*)

ELIZABETH BARROW COLT. (*Rigid with panic, muddles the timing of when to sit down, plops awkwardly. Sneaks out her glasses for another look, drops them back in her bag.*)

CAL. (*Pushing her the long distance to her table.*) Could I get you something to drink while you wait?

ELIZABETH BARROW COLT. (*Her sob again.*)

CAL. Something from the bar?

ELIZABETH BARROW COLT. (*Inaudible.*) What time is it?

CAL. I beg your pardon?

ELIZABETH BARROW COLT. (*Very shrill.*) TIME?

CAL. (*Startled, jumps, looks at his watch.*) 7:15.

ELIZABETH BARROW COLT. (*Faintly.*) I don't know what he looks like.

CAL. (*Leaning down close to her.*) I'm sorry . . .

ELIZABETH BARROW COLT. I've only talked to him on the phone.

CAL. (*Mystified.*) Could I get you something from the bar?

ELIZABETH BARROW COLT. How will I know him? (*Her sob.*)

CAL. Are you all right?

ELIZABETH BARROW COLT. (*Fishes in her pocketbook, hauls out a paperback edition of Thomas Mann's* The Magic Mountain, *opens it in the middle and starts reading, holding the book very close to her face.*) I brought my book . . .

CAL. How about a little appetizer or something while you wait?

ELIZABETH BARROW COLT. (*Keeps reading, making her little sob every now and then. She twists a strand of her hair.*)

CAL. He should be here any minute now . . . it's this awful weather . . . slows everyone down . . . cars won't start . . . batteries frozen up . . . he should be here any time now . . . worst winter we've had since I can remember . . .

PAUL. Waiter? Waiter, we're ready to order.

CAL. Would you excuse me, Mademoiselle? (*He heads towards the* GALTS' *table.*)

(*The light slowly fades on* ELIZABETH BARROW COLT.)

SCENE 4

And rise on ELLEN *who is holding a beautiful fresh bass.*

ELLEN. Just look at you, you sad beauty, you prehistoric fluke . . . where do you come from, anyway? All silver and slippery, with such a mournful face . . . (*She holds its face up to hers and imitates its pout.*) You don't even know you're a fish, do you? Aaaaaahhh, but *we* do . . . and we know how good you taste . . . oh yes . . . we know all about that . . . (*She starts sharpening her knife.*)

(*The light fades on her busy hands.*)

SCENE 5

And rise on CAL *hovering over the* GALTS.

PAUL. Hannah?

HANNAH. Oh Paul, I'm not ready!

PAUL. Take your time.

HANNAH. I keep changing my mind.

PAUL. There's no rush.

HANNAH. I'm so . . . tense.

PAUL. We have all the time in the world.

HANNAH. (*Motioning to* CAL.) The Belgian Oxtail Soup is . . .

CAL. A hearty beef broth with winter vegetables, smoked ham, and Madeira.

HANNAH. Madeira . . .

CAL. Madeira . . .

HANNAH. And the Billi Bi is . . .

CAL. A cream of mussel soup seasoned with fresh herbs, shallots, white wine, and a thread of saffron.

HANNAH. (*Impressed.*) . . . a thread of saffron . . .

CAL. Saffron . . .

HANNAH. And the Veal Prince Orloff is . . .

CAL. Roast veal stuffed with onions and wild mushrooms, served with Sauce Mornay . . .

HANNAH. (*Rolling it on her tongue.*) Sauce Mornay . . .

CAL. Sauce Velouté with Gruyere cheese added . . .

HANNAH. Sauce Velouté . . .

PAUL. Mornay!

HANNAH. And the roast duckling in wine with green grapes is . . .

CAL. Fresh.

HANNAH. Fresh!

HANNAH. And the Striped Bass with shrimp mousse . . . is . . .

CAL. In season!

HANNAH. In season!

PAUL. (*Grunts with anticipation.*)

HANNAH. Your vegetable of the day?

CAL. Braised celery.

PAUL. (*Kissing his fingers.*) My favorite! (*A silence.*)

HANNAH. Oh Paul!

PAUL. (*Reaching for her hand.*) Sssssshhhhh . . .

HANNAH. I'm just so . . .

PAUL. I know, I know . . .

HANNAH. I love roast duck!

CAL. The Duck is . . .

PAUL. I'm having the bass!

HANNAH. But I woke up with a craving for veal.

PAUL. I don't care for duck . . .

CAL. The veal is . . .

HANNAH. You know how I love veal!

PAUL. I had veal last week . . .

HANNAH. But I haven't had fresh roast duckling in . . .

CAL. You might like the bass . . .

PAUL. My rule of thumb: always order fish that's in season.

HANNAH. I only had an omelette for lunch.

CAL. The duckling is . . .

PAUL. I don't know about you, but I am starving!
HANNAH. I've been good all week.
PAUL. I can almost taste that mussel soup!

(*Faster and faster.*)

HANNAH. I've got to decide!
PAUL. I can't wait much longer . . .
HANNAH. I always have veal . . .
PAUL. I don't care for duck . . .
HANNAH. I could have the bass . . .
PAUL. I just want to start . . .
HANNAH. I need some more time . . .
PAUL. I can't wait much more . . .
HANNAH. I think I can go . . .
PAUL. I just want to . . .
HANNAH. I know I can . . .
PAUL. I . . .
HANNAH. I . . .
PAUL. (*In a burst.*) I'll have the Belgian Oxtail Soup to start, the Bass with Shrimp, and Floating Island for dessert! (*He pants slightly.*)

CAL. (*Writing it down.*) Very good, sir . . . and you, Madame?

HANNAH. (*Takes a deep breath, shuts her eyes, clenches her hands, pauses, then very fast.*) Billi Bi, Duckling in Wine with Green Grapes, and Pears in Cointreau with Frozen Cream.

PAUL. (*Applauds her.*) Nice going, Hannah! Very nice! Good work! (*He leans over the table and kisses her.*)

CAL. (*Writing it down.*) Yes, you did very well. (*He shakes her hand.*) Congratulations.

HANNAH. (*Eyes still shut, murmurs.*) Oh thank you, thank you, thank you so much . . .

CAL. (*Puts the last flourish on his pad and glides into the kitchen.*)

(*The light fades on the rhapsodic* GALTS.)

SCENE 6

ELLEN. (*Is more frantic than ever. She has several bass out and is dressing them.*)

CAL. (*Bursting in.*) One Oxtail . . . one Billi, one bass, one duck, one Floating Island, and one pears!

ELLEN. (*Eyes closed, reciting.*) One oxtail, one Billi, one bass, one duck, one Floating Island, and one pears . . .

CAL. One oxtail, one Billi, one bass, one duck, one Floating Island, and one pears . . . !

ELLEN. You do the shrimp and I'll do the eggs! (*She starts whipping egg whites with an automatic mixer . . . as.*)

CAL. (*Removes the shrimp from the refrigerator and dumps them into the Cuisinart. He turns it on. They both make a fearful clatter.*)

ELLEN. (*Over the din.*) Heavy cream!

CAL. How much?

ELLEN. Half a cup.

CAL. (*Starts pouring it into the Cuisinart.*) Watch . . .

ELLEN. That's enough. (*They finish their chores simultaneously.*) You slice the mushrooms and I'll finish the mousse! (*She pours the mousse out of the Cuisinart and carefully folds in the egg whites she's just whipped as . . .*)

CAL. (*Slices the mushrooms with lightning speed and precision.*)

ELLEN. You cut the grapes and I'll do the soups . . . (*She returns to her soups on the stove.*)

CAL. I'll cut the grapes . . .

ELLEN. While I do the soups . . .

CAL. Where are the grapes?

ELLEN. (*Muttering as she works on the soup.*) One Oxtail . . . one Billi, one bass, and one duck . . .

CAL. Where are the grapes?

ELLEN. Second shelf of the refrigerator.

CAL. Of course. (*Starts rooting around in the refrigerator.*)

ELLEN. One oxtail . . . one Billi, one bass, and one duck . . .

CAL. Second shelf.

ELLEN. That's right . . . (*Tastes the soup.*)

CAL. It's not there.

ELLEN. Then look in the bin . . .

CAL. (*Thumping around.*) Nope.

ELLEN. Try in the door.

CAL. (*Making more and more noise.*) Nothing.

ELLEN. Check the top shelf.

CAL. I already did.

ELLEN. They're not with the pears?

CAL. Not with the pears.

ELLEN. Not in the bin?

CAL. Not in the bin.

ELLEN. Start taking things out.

CAL. (*Does.*) I am!

ELLEN. They're not in the back?

CAL. Not . . . in . . . the back!

ELLEN. Under the bass?

CAL. Nowhere in sight!

ELLEN. Try by the cream.

CAL. I already have. (*He's now spread a great arc of food around the refrigerator.*)

ELLEN. They've got to be there.

CAL. Ellen, I'm looking!

ELLEN. Next to the stock.

CAL. Nowhere in sight!

ELLEN. Oh honey, I need them!

CAL. Yes, I know . . .

ELLEN. Should I come and help?

CAL. Son of a bitch!

ELLEN. I can't do the duck . . . (*Reaches for the salt and notices the bowl of empty grape stems.*) OH NO!

CAL. (*Picking over the mess strewn on the floor.*) They've got to be here!

ELLEN. *I DON'T BELIEVE THIS! (She lifts up the bowl to show* CAL.)

CAL. (*His back to her.*) I remember seeing them . . .

ELLEN. CAL, YOU ATE THEM!

CAL. (*His back to her, finds something tempting, starts eating it.*) Mmmmmmmm . . .

ELLEN. (*Holding up an empty branch.*) There's nothing left but the stems!

CAL. What *is* this?

ELLEN. LOOK!

CAL. (*Facing her.*) What?

ELLEN. You ate all the grapes.

CAL. No, I didn't. I didn't eat those.

ELLEN. (*Waving the branch.*) CAL!

CAL. I didn't eat any grapes.

ELLEN. I saw you!

CAL. Why would I eat those grapes?

ELLEN. I don't know, but I saw you!

CAL. I don't even like grapes.

ELLEN. I asked you to stop, don't you remember?

CAL. I'd never eat grapes.

ELLEN. CAL, YOU ATE THOSE GRAPES, I SAW YOU!

CAL. (*In a whisper.*) Not so loud, they'll hear you out front.

ELLEN. (*Whispering.*) How are we going to serve Duckling in Wine with Green Grapes?

CAL. I didn't do it.

ELLEN. You've ruined the dish.

CAL. You've made a mistake.

ELLEN. I can't go on like this . . .

CAL. Serve it with something else.

ELLEN. What's scarey is, you don't even know you're doing it.

CAL. Peaches or cherries.

ELLEN. It's like a disease . . .

CAL. Roast duck with Bing cherries is a classic!

ELLEN. YOU ATE THE BING CHERRIES THIS MORNING! (*She starts to cry.*)

CAL. Well, we have peaches don't we? Substitute peaches!

ELLEN. Cal, I can cook. I can *really* cook!

CAL. It's even better with peaches!

ELLEN. I could win us three stars, maybe even four!

CAL. (*Starts opening cupboard doors.*) Now where are those peaches?

ELLEN. I've trained with the best . . .

CAL. (*Thumping in one of the cupboards.*) I know they're in here somewhere . . .

ELLEN. . . . cooked with the best!

CAL. (*Finds a can of peaches.*) You see!

ELLEN. But I can't do this alone. I need you to help.

CAL. (*Starts opening the can.*) You golden babies . . .

ELLEN. You've always had such a keen palate.

CAL. (*The lid off, he inhales the fragrance, then reaches down for one, lifts it up, dripping and bright yellow. He pops it in his mouth.*)

ELLEN. . . . a razor sharp instinct. I need it, Cal!

CAL. There's nothing wrong with canned peaches, they're just as good as fresh. (*He then takes a swig of the juice.*) I don't know when I've tasted such a delicious peach . . .

ELLEN. Do you still have it? (*She rushes to a cupboard and sweeps down an armful of spice tins.*) SHOW ME IT'S THERE, SHOW ME YOUR TALENT! (*Concealing its identity, she pours out a heaping teaspoon of mustard and offers it to him.*) Taste this!

CAL. (*Offering her a large syruppy peach, still garbled.*) I really wish you'd try this, it's . . .

ELLEN. (*Fierce, forces the teaspoon of mustard into his mouth.*) *Taste!*

CAL. (*Spitting.*) What you are doing?

ELLEN. (*Shoveling in another batch.*) I SAID, TASTE IT!

CAL. (*Sputtering.*) Jesus, what is this?

ELLEN. You tell me, Cal!

CAL. (*Gagging.*) It's poison.

ELLEN. Try again!

CAL. (*Is certainly strong enough to overpower her, but it is food and he can't resist anything that's put into his mouth. Coughs.*)

ELLEN. What is it?

CAL. How am I supposed to tell, my mouth is on fire?!

ELLEN. Well, you'd better be able to tell if you want to stay in business, my dear! (*Forces in another spoonful.*)

CAL. (*Weakly.*) It's . . . curry powder!

ELLEN. Wrong!

CAL. Paprika . . .

ELLEN. Wrong!

CAL. Clove . . .

ELLEN. Wrong!

CAL. (*In pain.*) . . . Horse radish.

ELLEN. Think, Cal. Think!

CAL. Soy sauce?

ELLEN. Wrong!

CAL. Saffron?

ELLEN. Wrong!

CAL. Ginger?

ELLEN. Wrong!

CAL. (*With a sob.*) I don't know!

ELLEN. IT'S MUSTARD, CAL. SIMPLE MUS-TARD! (*She pours out another teaspoon of spice and puts it in his mouth.*) . . . and this?

CAL. (*Spits it out.*) Uuugh! You've gone crazy.

ELLEN. You don't know, do you!

CAL. Dill . . .

ELLEN. You're so glutted, you can't even tell . . . !

CAL. Cinnamon.

ELLEN. You can't even tell bitter from sweet.

CAL. Coffee?

ELLEN. It could be dirt for all you know! (*Shoves in another taste.*)

CAL. Nutmeg?

ELLEN. Unbelievable!

CAL. Anise? . . . Brown sugar? . . . Oregano? . . . Coriander? . . . Tarragon? . . .

ELLEN. It's salt, Cal.

(*The doorbell rings.*)

CAL. No!

ELLEN. What are we going to do?

CAL. It didn't taste anything like . . .

ELLEN. *Salt!*

CAL. (*Pouring some in his hand.*) Salt . . .

ELLEN. You drank all the Floating Island . . .

CAL. It didn't taste anything like salt!

ELLEN. You ate all the grapes . . .

CAL. (*Tastes the bit in his palm.*) Son of a bitch . . .

ELLEN. And now, canned peaches . . . *canned!*

CAL. You know, that is amazing. I never would have guessed it was . . . salt . . .

ELLEN. It makes no difference to you anymore. You'd eat *anything* and like it.

(*The doorbell rings again.*)

ELLEN. (*Goes back to stirring her Oxtail soup, tastes it, pours the remaining beaten egg yolk into the Billi Bi, tastes that, adding spices. She starts to cry.*) There's someone at the door, you'd better get it . . .

CAL. I'm sorry, El . . . I'll watch it from now on . . . I didn't realize . . .

ELLEN. (*Crying softly as she stirs the soup.*) I can't do it all by myself, I just can't . . . it's too hard . . . so much to do . . . I get lost sometimes, afraid I've done something wrong . . . I need you to help me . . . reassure me, Cal . . . tell me it's good . . . tell me it's fine . . . give me that strength . . . tell me it's fine . . .

CAL. (*Wraps his arms around her, rocks her.*) Ssssshhhh, come on El . . . it will be all right . . . we can still do it . . . we'll work it out . . . I'll watch the eating . . . they love you out there . . . they're breaking the doors down . . . listen to them . . . baby . . . baby . . . please . . .

(*The doorbell rings with strident insistence as . . .*)

THE CURTAIN SLOWLY FALLS

ACT TWO

SCENE 1

One hour later. A general view of the restaurant.
HANNAH *and* PAUL GALT *are lingering over their
desserts.* DAVID OSSLOW *has finally arrived and is
eating his soup as* ELIZABETH BARROW COLT
*stares at hers. The lights settle on the latest arrivals,
a trio of lively women in their 30's:* HERRICK
SIMMONS, *a hearty eater,* NESSA VOX, *a guilty
eater, and* TONY STASSIO, *a noneater who's on a
perpetual diet. A Teleman trio sonata plays softly,
then fades.*

HERRICK SIMMONS. (*Is looking at the wine list,
trying to make up her mind.*) Puligny-Montrachet!
(*Hands the list to* NESSA.)

NESSA VOX. (*Scanning it, considering.*) Puligny-
Montrachet . . . ?

TONY STASSIO. (*Takes the list from* NESSA *and
points.*) Pinot Chardonnay!

HERRICK SIMMONS. Pinot Chardonnay?

NESSA VOX. (*Takes the list from* TONY *and announces.*) Chateau de Lascombes!

HERRICK SIMMONS. Spare me! (*A pause.*)

CAL. (*Sensing trouble, comes to their table.*) Could
I be of any assistance?

TONY STASSIO. (*Taking the list back from* NESSA,
makes another choice. She knows nothing about wine.)
Cotes-du-Rhône!

CAL. Would you like a red wine or white?

TONY STASSIO. (*Pointing to another selection, mis-
pronouncing it.*) Chateauneuf-du-Papé!

44

CAL. A Burgundy or Beaujolais?

NESSA VOX. I'd like a chateau bottled red Bordeaux!

CAL. (*Making suggestions for her.*) Chateau Belgrave . . . Chateau La Lagune . . .

HERRICK SIMMONS. I think a white Burgundy would serve us much better.

CAL. (*Now to* HERRICK.) Pouilly Fuissé . . . Puligny-Montrachet . . .

TONY STASSIO. (*Stubborn.*) Nuits St. Georges!

CAL. (*Suggesting more Burgundies to* HERRICK.) Corton-Charlemagne . . .

TONY STASSIO. Pinot Chardonnay!

HERRICK SIMMONS. (*A tremendous sigh.*) Corton-Charlemagne, that's more like it!

TONY STASSIO. (*Has made up her mind, with stunning authority.*) PULIGNY-FUISSÉ!

CAL. (*Bewildered as no such brand exists.*) Puligny-Fuissé?

HERRICK SIMMONS, (*Trying to correct* TONY.) Puligny-*Montrachet!*

NESSA VOX. (*Likewise.*) Pouilly-Fuissé!

TONY STASSIO. (*More and more stubborn, more and more incorrect.*) Montrachet-Fuissé!

CAL. Montrachet-*Puligny!*

NESSA VOX. Puligny . . . Pouilly!

HERRICK SIMMONS. Pouilly-Fuissé!

CAL. Pouilly-Montrachet!

HERRICK SIMMONS. Pouilly-Montrachet?

NESSA VOX. Montrachet-Puligné (*Pronounced "Pulignay."*)

CAL. (*Repeating after her.*) Montrachet-Puligné!

HERRICK SIMMONS. (*Correcting his pronunciation.*) Nee!

CAL. (*Quickly, embarrassed.*) Nee!

TONY STASSIO. Montrachet-Romanee!

CAL. (*Correcting her pronunciation.*) Montrachet-Romané, *nay!*

TONY STASSIO. (*Triumphant in her ignorance.*) MONTRACHET-PULIGNAY!

CAL, HERRICK and NESSA. Nee, Nee! (*A pause.*)

HERRICK SIMMONS. (*Turns to* CAL *and gives him their order.*) Montrachet-Puligny!

CAL. (*Dutifully repeats after her.*) Montrachet-Puligny!

TONY STASSIO. (*Realizes they've reversed the order.*) Puligny-*Montrachet!*

CAL, HERRICK and TONY. (*All realize she's right and start laughing, repeating after her.*) Puligny-Montrachet! (*And the lights fade on them.*)

SCENE 2

And rise on ELIZABETH BARROW COLT *and* DAVID OSSLOW. ELIZABETH *is staring at her soup, motionless.* DAVID OSSLOW, *the successful head of his own publishing company, a man with a glowing appetite and glowing literary taste, is happily eating his. He's in his 50's, is dapper, at ease, and ready for anything.*

DAVID OSSLOW. I like your work very much.

ELIZABETH BARROW COLT. (*Drops her head and murmurs.*)

DAVID OSSLOW. We all like it . . .

ELIZABETH BARROW COLT. (*Shuts her eyes, murmurs again.*)

DAVID OSSLOW. I beg your pardon?

ELIZABETH BARROW COLT. (*Flinches.*)

DAVID OSSLOW. Are you all right?

ELIZABETH BARROW COLT. (*Nodding, eyes closed.*) Fine, fine, fine, fine, fine . . . (*A silence.*)

DAVID OSSLOW. For some reason I imagined you very differently. (*A silence.*) I thought you'd have a very large head.

ELIZABETH BARROW COLT. (*Starts laughing, wishing she could stop.*)

DAVID OSSLOW. No, really I did. I thought you'd have this . . . (*Indicating the size with his hands.*) huge head!

ELIZABETH BARROW COLT. (*Finds this hysterical, and trying not to laugh, makes peculiar squeaking sounds.*)

DAVID OSSLOW. You know how you form an image of someone you haven't met?

ELIZABETH BARROW COLT. (*Keeps laughing.*)

DAVID OSSLOW. I also pictured you as having very bushy eyebrows. You know, the kind that almost meet over the bridge of the nose . . .

ELIZABETH BARROW COLT. (*Helpless with laughter and embarrassment, tries to hide her face in her napkin and accidentally knocks over her bowl of soup, spilling the entire contents into her lap. She leaps to her feet, flapping like a wet puppy.*) Oh dear!

DAVID OSSLOW. (*Bolts out of his seat to help her.*) Are you all right?

ELIZABETH BARROW COLT. (*Frantically wiping at her dress with her napkin.*) I spilled . . .

DAVID OSSLOW. (*Lifting his napkin to help.*) Did you burn yourself?

ELIZABETH BARROW COLT. (*Shrinking from him.*) I spilled all my soup . . .

DAVID OSSLOW. (*Starts wiping at her dress with his napkin.*) Here, let me help . . .

ELIZABETH BARROW COLT. (*Turning her back to him.*) No, no, I can . . .

DAVID OSSLOW. Are you sure you're . . .

ELIZABETH BARROW COLT. I'm sorry . . .

DAVID OSSLOW. Let me get the waiter. Waiter!

ELIZABETH BARROW COLT. (*Her back turned, hunches over her spilled dress as if the most secret part of her body had suddenly sprung a leak.*) I can . . .

CAL. (*Striding over.*) Yes?

DAVID OSSLOW. I'm afraid we've had a slight spill. Could you please bring us some water and extra napkins?

ELIZABETH BARROW COLT. It's fine . . . it's coming right out . . . it's nothing . . . really nothing . . . (*Showing her dress.*) See, I got it all out . . .

CAL. Yes, right away, I'll get you some fresh napkins and we'll clean it up in no time! (*He produces several napkins from his pocket and joins DAVID OSSLOW in wiping ELIZABETH off.*)

ELIZABETH BARROW COLT. (*Dying of embarrassment since the spill hit her squarely in her crotch.*) No really I can . . . let me . . .

CAL. It shouldn't stain. A good dry cleaner should be able to get this right out . . . (*Feeling the material.*) What is the material, anyway? Cotton?

ELIZABETH BARROW COLT. It isn't my dress . . . (*She keeps fussing over it.*)

CAL. (*To DAVID OSSLOW, feeling the fabric.*) Wouldn't you say this was cotton?

DAVID OSSLOW. (*Feels it.*) No, that isn't cotton, it feels more like . . . rayon to me . . .

ELIZABETH BARROW COLT. (*Still wiping away.*) A friend lent it to me.

CAL. (*Feeling another section of it.*) Rayon? It's too light-weight to be rayon . . .

DAVID OSSLOW. It could be a wool challis . . .

CAL. I say it's either cotton or a cotton blend.

ELIZABETH BARROW COLT. I don't have a proper dress . . .

DAVID OSSLOW. As long as it's a synthetic, she should have no problems . . .

CAL. (*Feeling it again.*) You know, it might just be . . . silk!

DAVID OSSLOW. (*Feels.*) Silk?

CAL. That's right: silk!

DAVID OSSLOW. (*Still feeling.*) It certainly has the weight of silk . . .

CAL. It's silk! That's what it is!

ELIZABETH BARROW COLT. She'll kill me.

CAL. Don't worry, this will come right out. Silk sheds stains like water! (*Pushes into the kitchen with the soiled napkins.*)

DAVID OSSLOW. It's a nice dress.

ELIZABETH BARROW COLT. (*Trying to hide the immense stain with her napkin, heads back towards her chair.*) I'm sorry . . .

DAVID OSSLOW. (*Pulls out her chair for her.*) These kinds of things happen all the . . .

ELIZABETH BARROW COLT. (*Collapses in the chair before he's pulled it out all the way, making a loud plop.*) Oh dear, I . . .

DAVID OSSLOW. (*Strains to push the chair, with her in it, closer to the table.*) There we go . . . (*He returns to his seat, looks at her, reaches across the table and picks up her hand, squeezes it and then lets it go.*) Are you all right?

ELIZABETH BARROW COLT. (*Head down.*) Fine, fine, fine, fine fine . . . (*A silence.*)

CAL. (*Returns with a brand new bowl of steaming soup which he sets down before* ELIZABETH.) There we go! (*And he turns on his heel.*)

ELIZABETH BARROW COLT. (*Her shoulders giving way, looks at it.*) Oh dear. (*A slight pause.*)

DAVID OSSLOW. Elizabeth, I'd like to publish your short stories.

ELIZABETH BARROW COLT. (*Looking into the soup, stunned.*) Oh my.

DAVID OSSLOW. They're wonderful.

ELIZABETH BARROW COLT. Mercy!

DAVID OSSLOW. What did you say?

ELIZABETH BARROW COLT. (*Softly.*) I don't know what to say . . .

DAVID OSSLOW. . . . really wonderful!

ELIZABETH BARROW COLT. I never imagined . . . (*Starts fishing around in her pocketbook.*)

DAVID OSSLOW. You're incredibly gifted . . .

ELIZABETH BARROW COLT. Oh no, I'm . . . (*Pulls out her lipstick, lowers her head and sneaks on a smear, hands shaking. Suddenly she drops the lipstick. It falls into her soup with a splash.*) Oh no!

DAVID OSSLOW. What was that?

ELIZABETH BARROW COLT. (*Dives for it.*) Oh nothing, I just dropped my lipstick . . .

(*She repeatedly tries to retrieve it with her spoon, but it keeps splashing back down into her soup. She finally gives up, fishes it out with her hands, and drops it into her purse.*)

DAVID OSSLOW. Don't you like the soup?

ELIZABETH BARROW COLT. (*Hunched over her pocketbook.*) Oh yes, it's . . .

DAVID OSSLOW. It looks delicious.

ELIZABETH BARROW COLT. (*Staring at it.*) Yes, it's very nice.

DAVID OSSLOW. I've always loved French Provincial . . . I'm sorry . . . I . . .

ELIZABETH BARROW COLT. Would you like it?

(*A pause.*)

ELIZABETH BARROW COLT. OH, YOU HAVE IT!

DAVID OSSLOW. No, really, I . . .

ELIZABETH BARROW COLT. (*Picks up the bowl with trembling hands and starts lifting it across the table to him, her spoon still in it.*) I want you to have it!

DAVID OSSLOW. *Careful!*

ELIZABETH BARROW COLT. (*Giddy, the soup sloshing wildly.*) I never have soup!

DAVID OSSLOW. *LOOK OUT!*

ELIZABETH BARROW COLT. In fact, I hardly ever have dinner, either!

DAVID OSSLOW. Really, I . . .

ELIZABETH BARROW COLT. (*Sets it down in front of him, spilling some.*) THERE!

DAVID OSSLOW. (*Looks at it. Weakly.*) Well, thank you.

ELIZABETH BARROW COLT. (*Incredibly relieved, looks at him and sighs.*)

DAVID OSSLOW. (*Picks up her spoon and dips it into the soup.*)

ELIZABETH BARROW COLT. This is nice.

DAVID OSSLOW. (*Starts eating it.*)

ELIZABETH BARROW COLT. How is it?

DAVID OSSLOW. Very good. Would you like a taste?

ELIZABETH BARROW COLT. Oh, no thank you! (*A silence.*)

DAVID OSSLOW. Do you cook at all?

ELIZABETH BARROW COLT. Oh no.

DAVID OSSLOW. (*Reaches a spoonful of soup across the table to her.*) Come on, try some.

ELIZABETH BARROW COLT. (*She tastes it.*) My mother didn't cook either.

DAVID OSSLOW. Now isn't that good? (*Gives her another taste.*)

ELIZABETH BARROW COLT. Mmmmmmmm . . .
(*Quickly wipes her mouth with her napkin.*)

DAVID OSSLOW. (*Takes a taste himself.*) My mother
was a great cook.

ELIZABETH BARROW COLT. She didn't know how.
She grew up with servants.

DAVID OSSLOW. Her Thanksgiving dinners . . . !

ELIZABETH BARROW COLT. We had a cook. Lacey.
She was awful and she smelled.

DAVID OSSLOW. I cook every once in awhile.

ELIZABETH BARROW COLT. We all hated her. Especially my mother.

DAVID OSSLOW. My wife is a great cook! Some night
you'll have to come over for dinner! (*He settles into
his soup, eating with less and less relish as her story
progresses.*)

ELIZABETH BARROW COLT. In fact, when I was young
I never even saw my mother in the kitchen. The food
just appeared at mealtime as if by magic, all steaming
and ready to eat. Lacey would carry it in on these big
white serving platters that had a rim of raised china
acorns. Our plates had the same rim. Twenty-two acorns
per plate, each one about the size of a lump of chewed
gum. When I was very young I used to try and pry them
off with my knife . . . We ate every night at 8 o'clock
sharp because my parents didn't start their cocktail
hour until 7, but since dinner time was meant for ex-
changing news of the day, the emphasis was always on
talking . . . and not on eating. My father bolted his
food, and my mother played with hers: sculpting it up
into hills and then mashing it back down through her
fork. To make things worse, before we sat down at the
table she'd always put on a fresh smear of lipstick. I
still remember the shade. It was called, "Fire and Ice
. . ." a dark throbbing red that rubbed off on her fork
in waxy clumps that stained her food pink, so that by the

end of the first course she'd have rended everything into a kind of . . . rosy puree. As my father woolfed down his meat and vegetables, I'd watch my mother thread this puree through the raised acorns on her plate, fanning it out into long runny pink ribbons . . . I could never eat a thing . . . "WAKE UP, AMER-ICA!", she'd trumpet to me. "You're not being excused from this table until you clean up that plate!" So, I'd take several mouthfuls and then when no one was looking, would spit them out into my napkin. Each night I systematically transferred everything on my plate into that life-saving napkin . . .

DAVID OSSLOW. Jesus Christ.

ELIZABETH BARROW COLT. It's amazing they never caught on.

DAVID OSSLOW. (*Lights a cigarette and takes a deep drag.*)

ELIZABETH BARROW COLT. I mean, you'd think Lacey would have noticed the huge bundles of half chewed food I left in my chair . . .

DAVID OSSLOW. I have never had trouble eating!

ELIZABETH BARROW COLT. We used cloth napkins, afterall. They were collected after each meal.

DAVID OSSLOW. I can always eat, no matter where I am!

ELIZABETH BARROW COLT. We had a fresh one each evening.

DAVID OSSLOW. Believe me, I could use a little of your problem . . .

ELIZABETH BARROW COLT. Lacey washed and ironed them.

DAVID OSSLOW. That is, if you call not eating a problem.

ELIZABETH BARROW COLT. To launder them, she had to dump the food out.

DAVID OSSLOW. (*Patting his stomach.*) I should have such problems!

ELIZABETH BARROW COLT. She must have noticed. I left so much, at least a pound . . .

DAVID OSSLOW. I'm so bad, I start thinking about my next meal before I've even finished the one I'm eating!

ELIZABETH BARROW COLT. I wonder what she thought? If she was hurt that I could never get it down . . .

DAVID OSSLOW. Now *that's* serious . . . !

ELIZABETH BARROW COLT. I lived in constant fear that she'd tell my parents. You see I was terribly underweight . . .

DAVID OSSLOW. I love to eat!

ELIZABETH BARROW COLT. Or worse, that she'd sneak into my room some night, lugging all those bulging napkins . . . and spill everything out . . . from one end of my bed to the other . . . and *force* me to eat it . . .

DAVID OSSLOW. I've always loved to eat . . . It will be the death of me . . . Everytime I see my doctor, he says the same thing. He says, "David, you've got to lose some of that weight!" (*A silence.*)

ELIZABETH BARROW COLT. I used to bite my nails. I think it was because I was so hungry all the time.

DAVID OSSLOW. (*Hands her back her empty soup bowl.*) Thank you, it was delicious.

ELIZABETH BARROW COLT. (*Hiding her hands.*) I still bite them sometimes. (*A silence. She looks around the room, a sigh.*) This is wonderful. (*Another silence.*)

DAVID OSSLOW. Oh! I forgot to return your spoon! (*He hands it to her, covering her hand with both of his.*)

ELIZABETH BARROW COLT. (*Grasps it, turns it gently in her hands, sneaks it up against her cheek for a*

moment . . . and then drops it into her pocketbook.)
I can't believe this is happening. (*The lights fade.*)

SCENE 3

And rise on the entire restaurant and kitchen.

CAL. (*Is pouring the wine for* HERRICK.) Puligny
Montrachet.

ELLEN. (*Is fussing over her entrees.*) Ooooooooohhh-
hhhh!

HERRICK SIMMONS. (*Tasting the wine.*) Mmmmmm-
mmmm . . .

ELLEN. (*Inhaling the fragrance.*) Aaaaaaaahhhhhhhh!

HERRICK. (*Crooning over her wine in a different
register.*) Uuuuuuuuhhhhhh!

NESSA VOX. (*Eagerly, to* HERRICK.) How is it?

HANNAH. Oh Paul, that was . . .

ELLEN. Arrange the peach slices on the duck . . .

HERRICK SIMMONS. Symphonic!

HANNAH. . . . divine!

DAVID OSSLOW. (*To* ELIZABETH.) *That* . . . was
an outstanding soup!

ELLEN. (*Gazing at the veal*) . . . beautiful!

PAUL. Better than the Pavillion, better than the Tour
d'Argent . . .

CAL. (*Pouring wine for* NESSA.) Mademoiselle . . .

TONY STASSIO. I can hardly wait.

ELIZABETH BARROW COLT. I wasn't sure how to get
here . . .

ELLEN. . . . ladle the Mornay on the veal . . .

NESSA VOX. (*Tastes her wine and makes little
mewing sounds.*)

HANNAH. . . . better than *any* meal I've had anywhere . . .

ELLEN. (*Handling the duck.*) . . . inspired!

PAUL. Here, here . . .

TONY STASSIO. (*Grabs* NESSA'S *hand.*) I'm going to have a heart attack!

ELLEN. (*Fussing over the bass.*) Yes, my little bass . . .

PAUL. The best . . . !

TONY STASSIO. (*Her hand on her heart.*) No, really, I am!

HANNAH. Well, Ken and Diva did rave, remember?

NESSA VOX. (*To* TONY.) Just don't keel over until the food comes!

DAVID OSSLOW. In fact, *both* soups were outstanding!

ELLEN. (*Inhaling the bass.*) Devastating . . .

ELIZABETH BARROW COLT. (*To* DAVID.) I almost got on the wrong bus.

HERRICK SIMMONS, (*Raises her glass to her friends.*) To the meal!

NESSA VOX. To the meal!

TONY STASSIO. To the meal!

CAL. (*Dives back into the kitchen, to* ELLEN.) They can hardly wait!

ELLEN. (*Has put the final touches on her entrees.*) All set . . .

CAL. (*Hoists the tray over his head.*) So far . . . so good . . . (*And plunges back into the dining room.*)

ELLEN. (*As he disappears.*) So far . . . so good.

CAL. (*Glides towards the womens' table with his tray.*)

HERRICK SIMMONS. (*Catching sight of the food.*) Oooooooohhhhhh!

NESSA VOX. Aaaaaaaahhhhhhhhhhh!

TONY STASSIO. Mmmmmmmmmmmmmmmmmm!

CAL. (*Sets his tray down on a folding waiter's table. Picks up the duckling and sets it down before* HERRICK.) Duckling in wine with . . . sliced peaches!

TONY STASSIO. Ohhhh, look!

NESSA VOX. It's a masterpiece! Look at the color of those peaches . . . pure Cezanne!

TONY STASSIO. Sir, I think you made a mistake, *I* was the one who ordered . . . (*She starts to reach for the duck but is stopped as.*)

CAL. (*Sets down the veal at her place. Each dish he presents is more spectacular than the last one.*) . . . and for Mademoiselle, Veal Prince Orloff!

TONY STASSIO. (*Stops her hana's flight towards the duck and gasps.*) Yessss!

NESSA VOX. (*Staring at it.*) My God!

HERRICK SIMMONS. (*Weakly.*) Do you see that . . . stuffing?

NESSA VOX. It's . . . overwhelming! Absolutely . . .

TONY STASSIO. (*Looking down at it, very pleased.*) Perfect!

HERRICK SIMMONS. Do you smell that sauce? That's Sauce Velouté! . . . Phillip's favorite!

NESSA VOX. I think I'm going to die!

HERRICK SIMMONS. I'd know it anywhere!

NESSA VOX. (*To* TONY.) I thought you wanted the duck.

HERRICK SIMMONS. No, she ordered the bass. He made a mistake, the veal is mine!

TONY STASSIO. I didn't order bass!

NESSA VOX. (*To* CAL.) Excuse me, Sir, but I believe that veal belongs to *me!*

HERRICK SIMMONS. (*Holding out her plate of duck.*) Who ordered this duck?

TONY STASSIO. I'd never order bass with shrimp, I'm on a diet!

HERRICK SIMMONS. That veal is mine!

TONY STASSIO. (*To* HERRICK.) The *duck* is yours!

NESSA VOX. (*To* TONY.) I thought the duck was *yours!*

HERRICK SIMMONS. No, it's *hers!* (*Indicating* NESSA). The veal is mine.

NESSA VOX. Then who ordered the bass?

HERRICK SIMMONS. (To TONY.) You did.

TONY STASSIO. (Indicating NESSA.) She did!

CAL. (*Sets the bass down before* NESSA. *It's the triumph of the three dishes. They all want it.* CAL *exits.*)

NESSA VOX. (*Gasps.*) My God!

TONY STASSIO. (*Reaches for the bass.*) No, no, *that's* mine! *I* ordered the bass!

HERRICK SIMMONS. (*Snatches the bass out from under* NESSA *and gives* NESSA *her duck in exchange. To* TONY.) Oh no you didn't!

NESSA VOX. (*Looking at the duck.*) Hey, where's my bass?

TONY STASSIO. (*Grabs the bass away from* HERRICK *and gives her the veal in exchange.*) Now, wait just one minute!

NESSA VOX. I didn't order duck!

HERRICK SIMMONS. . . . and I didn't order veal!

TONY STASSIO. (*Starts to eat the bass.*) Mmmmmm-mmmmm . . .

NESSA VOX. (*Pulls the bass away from* TONY *and gives her the duck.*) HEY, YOU CAN'T EAT THAT BASS. IT'S MINE!

HERRICK SIMMONS. (*To* TONY.) You ordered the duck, don't you remember?

TONY STASSIO. (*Handing* NESSA HERRICK'S *veal.*) *She* ordered the veal . . . (*Handing* HERRICK NESSA'S *duck.*) *You* ordered the duck . . . and (*Taking* NESSA'S *bass.*) I ordered the bass!

NESSA VOX. I would never order veal!

HERRICK SIMMONS. You think I'd order . . . *duck?*

TONY STASSIO. Of course you'd order duck! (*This entree snatching speeds up into a whirlwind.*)

HERRICK SIMMONS. (*Taking the bass from* TONY *and giving her the duck in exchange.*) That is, if *you* hadn't ordered it first!

NESSA VOX. (*Totally confused, to* HERRICK.) I thought you wanted the veal.

TONY STASSIO. (*Takes* NESSA's *veal and gives it to* HERRICK . . . *then takes* HERRICK's *bass and gives* NESSA *the duck.*) Yes! (*To* HERRICK.) You did!

NESSA VOX. Then who ordered the bass?

HERRICK SIMMONS. (*Grabs the bass back from* TONY *and gives her the veal in exchange.*) I did!

NESSA VOX. Oh, no you didn't . . . this bass is mine! (*She takes the bass from* HERRICK *and gives her the duck.*)

TONY STASSIO. NO, THE VEAL IS YOURS! (*She gives* NESSA *the veal and snatches the bass.*) IT'S MY BIRTHDAY, SO THE BASS IS MINE! (*She starts eating the bass. Silence.*)

HERRICK SIMMONS. (*To* NESSA.) She's eating all my bass!

NESSA VOX. Well, you're eating all her duck! (*Raises her glass to* TONY.) Happy Birthday!

HERRICK SIMMONS. (*Likewise.*) Happy Birthday!

DAVID OSSLOW. Waiter, the wine list please.

(*The three women start eating with gusto, save* TONY *who takes tiny bites. As* CAL *passes, he croons in shared delight.*)

TONY STASSIO. (*To* NESSA.) How's the veal, it looks delicious.

(*They continue to eat.*)

TONY STASSIO. (*Suddenly pushes her bass away.*) I don't know about you two, but I am stuffed!

NESSA VOX. But we've hardly started . . .

TONY STASSIO. Can't . . . eat . . . another . . . bite!

HERRICK SIMMONS. You ought to taste this duck, it's heaven!

TONY STASSIO. I think I'm going to burst.

NESSA VOX. Tony, you haven't eaten anything!

HERRICK SIMMONS. (*Offering* TONY *a forkful of bass.*) Come on, try it . . .

TONY STASSIO. (*Shaking her head.*) Really, I'm . . .

NESSA VOX. (*Lays down her fork.*) I don't believe this!

HERRICK SIMMONS. (*Plows into her bass with renewed vigor.*) Well, you're missing something fabulous!

NESSA VOX. (*To* HERRICK.) She says she's finished . . .

HERRICK SIMMONS. Mmmmmmm!

NESSA VOX. Look at her plate!

TONY STASSIO. Don't let me spoil your dinner just because I'm dieting . . .

HERRICK SIMMONS. Aaaaaaahhhhhh!

NESSA VOX. She hasn't touched it.

HERRICK SIMMONS. Nessa, you've got to try some of this duck. (*Offers her a forkful.*)

TONY STASSIO. You two just go right ahead . . .

NESSA VOX. Well if she's not going to eat, then neither am I!

HERRICK SIMMONS. (*Offering* NESSA *the duck more forcefully.*) Come on, it's sensational!

NESSA VOX. (*Tastes it.*) Mmmmmmmmmmm!

HERRICK SIMMONS. Isn't that something?

TONY STASSIO. (*Lifting up her plate.*) Would anyone like my bass?

HERRICK SIMMONS. (*Giving* NESSA *another bite.*) And now taste it with some of the peaches . . .

NESSA VOX. (*Does.*) MY GOD!

HERRICK SIMMONS. Hmmm?

NESSA VOX. (*Flutters.*)

TONY STASSIO. I've already lost four pounds this week!

NESSA VOX. TONY, YOU'VE GOT TO TRY THIS DUCK, YOU'LL DIE!

HERRICK SIMMONS. (*Reaching a forkful over to* TONY.) It's unbelievable . . .

NESSA VOX. It's the best duck I've ever . . .

HERRICK SIMMONS. Here, let me get you more sauce. (*She offers* TONY *a heaping spoonful.*)

NESSA VOX. You won't know what hit you!

TONY STASSIO. (*Shielding her mouth with her hand.*) No really, I couldn't . . .

NESSA VOX. (*To* HERRICK.) Wouldn't you say that was the best duck you've ever . . .

TONY STASSIO. (*Trying to ward them off.*) Please . . .

HERRICK SIMMONS. (*More threatening with her fork.*) Just a little taste . . . !

NESSA VOX. Come on, it won't kill you!

HERRICK SIMMONS. Open!

NESSA VOX. (*Scoops some up with her fork and also menaces* TONY *with it.*) We insist!

HERRICK SIMMONS. It really is . . .

NESSA VOX. Quite . . .

TONY STASSIO. Please!

NESSA VOX. Wonderful.

TONY STASSIO. Don't . . .

HERRICK SIMMONS. You should . . .

TONY STASSIO. . . . force me!

HERRICK SIMMONS. . . . try it!

NESSA VOX. Come on, Tony! You promised . . .

HERRICK SIMMONS. Eat the duck!

NESSA VOX. You've hardly eaten anything.

TONY STASSIO. I've got to lose ten more pounds!

NESSA VOX. (*Dumps the duck off her fork and threatens* TONY *with some of her veal.*) At least try the veal!

TONY STASSIO. (*Shielding her face with both hands.*) Only 10 pounds! (*She starts to cry.*)

NESSA VOX. (*Slams down her fork.*) FUCK IT THEN. JUST FUCK IT! (*Silence.*)

HERRICK SIMMONS. (*Resumes eating her duck.*) Ignore her.

NESSA VOX. HOW CAN I IGNORE HER WHEN WE'RE SITTING AT THE SAME TABLE AND SHE REFUSES TO EAT?!

HERRICK SIMMONS. It's her problem. (*Offering* NESSA *another forkful of duck.*) Come on, help me with this duck.

TONY STASSIO. I'm fat.

NESSA VOX. She says she's fat!

HERRICK SIMMONS. (*Reaching across for a taste of* NESSA's *veal.*) How's your veal?

TONY STASSIO. (*Lifts up her arm, pulls the under part of it.*) Look at that!

NESSA VOX. That isn't fat! That's your arm!

HERRICK SIMMONS. (*Eating* NESSA's *veal.*) Mmmm-mmm! Very nice!

TONY STASSIO. It's fat.

NESSA VOX. (*Lifts up her plate of veal and gives it to* HERRICK.) Here, have it all, I don't want any.

HERRICK SMITH. Don't give it all to me!

TONY STASSIO. (*Gives* HERRICK *her bass.*) You can have my bass too.

NESSA VOX. She ruined the whole meal.

HERRICK SIMMONS. I can't eat all of this! (*As she starts to do just that.*)

TONY STASSIO. (*Smiling, to* NESSA.) How was the veal?

NESSA VOX. You'd think I'd learn . . .

HERRICK SIMMONS. What's going on here?

TONY STASSIO. (*To* NESSA, *referring to the veal.*) It looks good.

NESSA VOX. She does it every time!

TONY STASSIO. (*To* HERRICK.) And your bass looks really . . .

NESSA VOX. IT'S NOT AS IF SHE EVER STICKS TO ANY OF HER DIETS! AS SOON AS SHE GETS HOME, SHE'LL OPEN UP THE REFRIGERATOR AND HAVE HERSELF ONE WHALLOPING OR GY . . . !

HERRICK SIMMONS. Take it easy . . .

NESSA VOX. SHE DENIES HERSELF IN FRONT OF US, BUT OH, WHEN SHE GETS INTO THE PRIVACY OF HER OWN REFRIGERATOR . . .

TONY STASSIO. (*Hands over her ears.*) I don't know what she's talking about . . .

HERRICK SIMMONS. (*To* NESSA.) Come on . . .

NESSA VOX. DOES SHE EVER GO AT IT! I know her. (*To* HERRICK.) Would you like to hear?

HERRICK SIMMONS. Nessa, don't . . .

NESSA VOX. First . . . just to warm up, she woolfs down a Twin Pack of Golden Ridges Potato Chips followed by a fistful of Nabisco Nilla Wafers. Then, it's on to the freezer for the real stuff: Hungry Man TV dinners flash frozen by Swansons, Howard Johnson's, Stouffers, Mortons, Mrs. Paul, Ronzoni, and Chun King! . . . But . . . can she wait for them to heat up? . . . God knows, it's a long wait for a Hungry Man TV dinner when you're languishing for it . . . the piquant steak in onion gravy, the hashed brown potato nuggets, the peas and carrots in seasoned sauce, and the delectible little serving of apple cake cobbler, pristine and golden in its tidy aluminum compartment . . . So, while it's warming at 400 degrees, she'll help herself to some Pepperidge Farm corn muffins, fully baked and ready to serve. Still frozen, mind you . . . still frosted with a thin sheen of ice, but there's nothing wrong with eating frozen corn muffins . . . especially if you turn out the lights and eat them in the dark . . . lift them up to your mouth . . . in the dark . . . roll your tongue over them . . . in the . . .

HERRICK SIMMONS. NESSA, THAT'S ENOUGH! (*A silence.*)

TONY STASSIO. (*Trying to recover, in a quavering voice.*) Well, I wonder if it's warmed up at all outside . . . (*She wets her finger and rubs it around the rim of her glass making eerie music. Another silence.*)

HERRICK SIMMONS. (*Pushing her bass away.*) Well, I guess I'm done. Anyone want the rest of this food?

TONY STASSIO. It's actually dangerous to go out on a night like this . . . (*A silence.*)

NESSA VOX. Well, if you two are finished, then so am I . . . (*Pushes her veal towards the center of the table.*)

HERRICK SIMMONS. . . . can't eat another bite!

TONY STASSIO. I don't know when I've been so full!

NESSA VOX. If I have one more taste, I'm going to explode!

HERRICK SIMMONS. You're going to explode! What about me? I won't be able to fit behind the wheel of the car to drive us home! (*This gets slower and slower.*)

TONY STASSIO. I can't go on . . .

NESSA VOX. I've had it . . .

HERRICK SIMMONS. I am stuffed!

TONY STASSIO. I can't move . . .

NESSA VOX. I'm in pain!

HERRICK SIMMONS. I feel sick . . .

TONY STASSIO. I'm . . . dying . . . (*The lights fade around them.*)

SCENE 4

And rise on PAUL *and* HANNAH GALT. *They have just been presented with snifters of after dinner brandy.*

PAUL. (*Picks his up and sloshes it around, inhaling the fragrance.*)

HANNAH. (*Does the same, then holds out her glass to* PAUL.) A toast!

PAUL. (*Offering her his glass.*) Oh good, I love toasts!

HANNAH. (*Clinking his glass.*) To . . . us! (*She drinks.*)

PAUL. (*Drinks.*) That's very sweet, Hannah.

HANNAH. (*Reaches out her glass and clinks his again.*) You and me all the way. (*She drinks.*)

PAUL. (*Drinks again.*) Here, here! (*A silence.*)

HANNAH. (*Lifts up her glass again.*) I want to make another toast!

PAUL. You're on!

HANNAH. (*Clinking his glass.*) To our wonderful children . . . Brian and Michelle! (*She drinks.*)

PAUL. Brian and Michelle . . . super kids! (*He drinks.*)

HANNAH. Gee, I'm having a good time. (*She kicks off her shoes. A silence.*)

PAUL. (*Leans back in his chair, swirling his brandy.*) This is very pleasant . . . very pleasant indeed.

HANNAH. (*Leaning forward.*) Another toast!

PAUL. Not again!

HANNAH. (*Clinking his glass.*) Oh come on, Paul . . . toast!

PAUL. (*Clinks with her.*) Toast.

HANNAH. Guess.

PAUL. What do you mean, "guess?"

HANNAH. Guess what I'm going to toast.

PAUL. Hannah, I couldn't possibly *guess* . . .

HANNAH. Of course you can, just try . . .

PAUL. (*Raising his glass.*) To . . . Oh, Hannah, we could sit here all night, there's no way I could *guess* what you're . . .

HANNAH. Alright, alright! I thought you could guess, but if you can't . . . you can't! (*A pause, she lifts her glass, clinks it to his.*) To your long and curly eyelashes!

PAUL. (*Pulls back his glass.*) To my . . . long and curly *eyelashes???!*

HANNAH. Yes, they're gorgeous! (*She drinks again.*)

PAUL. (*In a whisper.*) Hannah, I can't drink to my . . . *eyelashes!*

HANNAH. Well, I can . . . and I'm going to because they're gorgeous!

PAUL. They are?

HANNAH. Very long . . . and very curly!

PAUL. You never told me that before.

HANNAH. Well, I'm telling you now . . .

PAUL. (*Studies his reflection in his brandy glass.*) Son of a bitch!

HANNAH. (*Getting tipsy, clinking his glass again.*) Toast . . . toast!

PAUL. Not so loud.

HANNAH. (*Clanks softer.*) Sorry . . .

PAUL. (*Still peering at his reflection in his glass.*) They're really long and curly?

HANNAH. (*Touching his glass.*) Toast, toast! . . . To your knee caps! You have fabulous knee caps! (*She drinks.*)

PAUL. (*Looks around the room, embarrassed.*) Hannah!

HANNAH. Come on, drink!! (*She drinks again.*)

PAUL. (*In a whisper.*) Not to my *knee caps,* for Christsakes!

HANNAH. (*Raps his glass again.*) TO ONE . . . STUNNING PAIR OF KNEE CAPS! (*She drinks.*)

PAUL. (*Embarrassed, laughs.*) Hannah, stop it!

HANNAH. Really . . . *stunning!*

(*A few of the diners look over at them.*)

PAUL. OK . . . if that's the way you want to play . . . (*He holds out his glass to her.*) I would like to propose a toast!

HANNAH. (*Sitting back in her chair.*) Oh goody! (*She offers her glass.*)

PAUL. To your snowy white thighs! (*He clinks and drinks.*)

HANNAH. (*Snatches her glass away, embarrassed.*) Paul!

PAUL. (*Clinking her glass again.*) May they continue to bewitch and excite . . . (*He drinks.*)

HANNAH. (*In a hiss.*) Paul, stop it, it's not funny! . . . People are looking!

(HERRICK, NESSA, *and* TONY *stare openly and try not to laugh.*)

PAUL. (*Directly to them.*) Well, it's true, she's got one terrific pair of snowy white thighs!

HANNAH. (*Dying of embarrassment.*) I don't believe this . . .

PAUL. Would I lie?

HANNAH. (*In a dry whisper.*) Paul, stop it! Just . . . stop it!

PAUL. (*Stands and toasts everyone in the room.*) Well, bon appetit to one and all. (*He drinks, then sits back down.*)

HANNAH. I've never been so embarrassed . . .

PAUL. Oh, come on Hannah, we're just fooling around . . .

HANNAH. Maybe *you're* fooling around, but *I'm* not . . . !

PAUL. So, all of a sudden *I'm* fooling around, is that it . . . ?

HANNAH. You brought it up, not me!

PAUL. You think I'm fooling around, is that what you're saying?

HANNAH. I never said you were fooling around . . . *you* said *we* were just fooling around.

PAUL. Are you fooling around?

HANNAH. What do you mean, am *I* fooling around? What kind of a question is that?

PAUL. *Are* you fooling around?

HANNAH. (*After a pause.*) Well, I'm not telling.

PAUL. You mean, you are fooling around?

HANNAH. What do you think?

PAUL. Frankly, I don't know what to think!

HANNAH. Well, neither do I . . . I mean, what a thing to ask me after a nice dinner and everything . . .

PAUL. (*Putting his hand over hers.*) I'm sorry.

HANNAH. (*Sulking.*) So am I . . .

PAUL. (*After a pause.*) Forgive me?

HANNAH. I have to think about it. (*A silence as they both sip their brandies.*)

PAUL. Have you thought about it yet?

HANNAH. Maybe.

PAUL. Would you care to tell me what you decided?

HANNAH. That depends . . .

PAUL. Yes?

HANNAH. Do you promise never to embarrass me in public again?

PAUL. I promise.

HANNAH. Cross your heart?

PAUL. (*Crosses his heart.*) Cross my heart! (*Then lifts his glass to hers.*) I'll never embarrass you in public again! (*He drinks.*)

HANNAH. (*She drinks, mournful.*) I'm not fooling around. (*A silence.*)

PAUL. (*Eager, reaches his glass forward.*) A toast, another toast!

HANNAH. (*Offering her glass.*) Yes?

PAUL. To our next meal! (*He clinks.*)

HANNAH. Oh, I like that!

PAUL. (*Drinks.*)

HANNAH. That's more like it. (*She drinks.*) To our next meal. (*And leans over and kisses him.*)

(*The lights fade.*)

SCENE 5

And rise on ELLEN *and* CAL *in the kitchen. The food that* ELLEN *was working with in the first act has multiplied, tenfold. It's tumbling off the counters and overflowing on the stove.* ELLEN *and* CAL *race in the midst of it like figures in a speeded up old time movie.*

ELLEN. (*Is adding raw mushrooms and spices to a salad. She then tosses it, all the while talking on the telephone which she has tucked under her chin.*) COULD YOU SPEAK INTO THE PHONE A LITTLE LOUDER, PLEASE? I'M HAVING TROUBLE HEARING

CAL. (*Prepares a tray of coffee, cups, sugar, cream, and silverware for the* GALTS, *all the while talking on the other telephone which he has tucked under his chin.*) No, nothing pleases us more than hearing from satisfied customers, you're not bothering us in the

YOU. YES . . . THAT'S MUCH BETTER. Now, you were saying, you'd like reservations for how many? Three for Thursday the 9th . . . I'm sorry, we're completely filled the 9th. Could I suggest Tuesday the 14th . . . ? I SAID, TUESDAY THE 14TH! Yes, that's right, you could choose any time you like. I BEG YOUR PARDON? SOFT SHELLED CRABS? Yes, I agree with you, they are delicious . . . yes . . . yes . . . No, I WOULDN'T DREAM OF DEEP FRYING THEM, I NEVER DEEP FRY ANYTHING . . . Yes, yes . . . you'd like to call me back after you've talked it over with your husband? Fine . . . I SAID, THAT WOULD BE FINE. THANK YOU FOR CALLING. Goodbye. (*She hangs up.*)

least . . . You've never tasted such inspired Chicken Kiev in your life? ELLEN, THEY'VE NEVER TASTED SUCH INSPIRED CHICKEN KIEV IN THEIR LIVES! And you'd like to come back for more? We change our menu every day, you realize, so I couldn't guarantee you that same Chicken Kiev again . . . Now, which evening were you thinking of coming back? Thursday the 9th at 7:30? Yes, that would be fine . . . your name please? Kipner? . . . OH YES, OF COURSE, I REMEMBER YOU FROM LAST WEEK. YOU WERE THE PARTY OF FOUR WHO ORDERED EXTRA SALADS. Well, thank you for calling. We'll see you on the 9th. Goodbye. (*He hangs up.*)

ELLEN. That was three for the 14th . . . maybe.

CAL. Six for the 9th . . . ?

ELLEN. Six for the 9th? We're filled on the 9th!

CAL. You said, fourteen on the 3rd?

ELLEN. You should have made it for the 18th. The salads are ready to go. (CAL *exits to the dining room with the salads.*) We have plenty of room on the 18th. He could have made it for the 21st which is a holiday . . . (*Turning towards her sauce and picking up three eggs.*) And now for my hollandaise, my thick and rich hollandaise for the bass! (*She separates the eggs for the Hollandaise Sauce.*)

CAL. (*Careening back into the kitchen.*) 14 on the 3rd is fantastic. That's what I like to hear: *big numbers.* 14 on the 3rd . . . 19 on the 10th . . . 25 on the 16th!

ELLEN. (*Beating the yolks.*) Slow down. It's not 14 on the 3rd. It's 3 on the 14th, but we're talking about the 9th, and we're filled on the 9th!

CAL. (*Fussing with his coffee tray.*) We can divide them up into two tables of seven . . .

ELLEN. We have plenty of room on the 18th! Vinegar . . . (*She adds a drop.*)

CAL. . . . or three tables of five minus one . . .

ELLEN. I could handle four on the 18th . . .

CAL. How about one table of six and two tables of four?

ELLEN. Or even five on the 19th . . . salt . . . (*She adds a pinch.*)

CAL. Or . . . four tables of three . . .

ELLEN. . . . but six on the 9th? . . . Impossible!

CAL. (*As he plunges into the dining room with his tray of coffees.*) No problem!

ELLEN. Pepper! MY BASS! (*She rushes to the oven and pulls out her bass, takes the lid off.*) Oh, just look how lovely you are! And how delicious you smell . . . a garden full of herbs . . . perfect! (*She puts the bass on a counter top.*)

CAL. (*Popping back into the kitchen.*) Baby, we are going to expand!

ELLEN. OH NO WE'RE NOT! Fish juices. (*She pours off the fish juices into her Hollandaise.*)

CAL. We are going to build onto the side of the house . . .

ELLEN. Over my dead body! Heavy cream. (*She beats in the heavy cream.*)

CAL. Enclose the back yard . . .

ELLEN. Just try it . . . twelve tablespoons of melted butter. Smooth and easy. Come on baby . . .

CAL. (*Refilling the water pitcher.*) Break through the bedroom. . .

ELLEN. (*Beats and grunts.*)

CAL. Knock out those back walls.

ELLEN. Cal, you're losing your mind! Raving like a madman.

CAL. Add a good 200 feet.

ELLEN. NO!

CAL. If we use our heads, Ellen, we can fit fifty more tables in there! (*He rushes back to the dining room to pour the ladies their wine and deposit his water pitcher.*)

ELLEN. The next time he comes through that door, he'll announce we're opening a franchise! (*She returns to her sauce with a joyous fury.*) Oh yes . . . you little yellow sweetheart . . . you thick and creamy love of mine . . . you luscious baby . . . thicken! . . . Break through the bedroom . . . ?! Thaaaaat's the way . . . you're doing fine . . . oh yes . . . just fine . . . you tangy heartbreaker, you zesty tease . . . fifty more tables? . . . NEVER!

(*She dances around the kitchen whipping her sauce.*)

CAL. (*Comes careening back*) With a little planning, we could be feeding 200 people a night!

ELLEN. Not in this house! Not in *my* restaurant! (*She gives the sauce one more stroke and sets it aside on the counter.* EVERYTHING'S GOING TO BE FINE! Lemon juice . . . (*She adds a final drop of lemon juice.*)

CAL. That's over $5,000! (*He eyes the Hollandaise she's just made.*)

ELLEN. Just . . . fine!

CAL. (*Reaches for a spoon and unconsciously scoops out a taste of the Hollandaise.*) $5,000 a night, comes to $30,000 a week!

ELLEN. (*Turns to the wild rice simmering on another burner, stirs it, adjusting the seasoning.*) They'll love it!

CAL. At that rate we could pay back our loan within six months!

ELLEN. They'll die over it!

CAL. We'd be in the clear . . . (*He takes another taste of the sauce. ELLEN has planted a decoy pan of lemon yogurt for CAL to drink so the actor won't die of heartburn, she simply switches pans at the last minute.*)

ELLEN. Oh Cal, I want them to die over it!

CAL. If we could just pay off that loan . . . (*He picks up the saucepan of Hollandaise and starts drinking it.*)

ELLEN. (*Her back to him as she dishes out the rice.*) I am a cook who takes chances!

CAL. (*Gulping it down.*) Ellen, I gave up my law practice for this!

ELLEN. (*Transferring the bass to a serving platter.*) . . . a cook . . . who delivers!

CAL. Eight years of a successful business!

ELLEN. (*Smells the bass, tastes the drippings.*) . . . and I keep getting better!

CAL. (*Starts to spill the sauce down his front.*) A lot of people told me I was crazy. . . *you* even told me I was crazy. . . give up an assured annual income of 90 thousand and go 75 thousand into debt. . . for what?

ELLEN. (*One more taste.*) It's . . . perfect!

CAL. To open a restaurant in our living room!

ELLEN. (*Croons over the bass.*)

CAL. Insanity!

ELLEN. (*Reaches for her sauce.*) And now for the crowning glory . . . my sauce . . . my Hollandaise . . .

CAL. A wonderful little restaurant that would serve out of this world food . . . an old dream of ours . . .

ELLEN. (*Her back to him, scans the counter top.*) Now where did I put it? I just had it . . .

CAL. You could cook to your heart's content . . .

ELLEN. Damn!

CAL. I could run the place, show off my entreprenurial skills . . .

ELLEN. Where's my sauce?

CAL. *But we'd have to be serious about it and make some money!* I'm having trouble sleeping at night!

ELLEN. (*Finally sees him with the pan.*) Oh Cal! You . . . *can't* . . . you . . . *didn't!*

(*She staggers to the stove.*)

CAL. (*Stops drinking, unaware of his action.*)

ELLEN. (*Blindly rushes to him and tries to wrest the pan from his hands.*) HOW . . . COULD . . . YOU . . . *DRINK* . . . HOLLANDAISE SAUCE??? . . . THE *TASTE*, CAL . . .

CAL. (*Trying to ward her off.*) Hey, take it easy . . .

ELLEN. How could you just take it off the burner. . . pick up the pan. . . and drink out of it? (*She starts swatting him with a towel.*)

CAL. Watch it!

ELLEN. You're like some animal . . . an animal drinking out of its trough . . .

CAL. (*As the sauce sloshes wildly.*) Look out!

ELLEN. (*She finally wrenches it from him . . . holds the pan aloft and with deadly calm, pours it on the floor.*) Go on, Cal, drop down to the floor and lap it up! Lower your muzzle into it . . . *and drink!*

(She pushes him from behind.)

CAL. *(Loses his balance and sprawls on his hands and knees into the sauce...he backs away from it, horrified.)*

ELLEN. *(In a towering rage.)* THAT DOES IT, I'M SORRY, BUT . . . *THAT DOES IT!!!*

(She starts hurling pots and pans into the sink. She picks up whatever is big and makes noise and throws it across the room. She then pulls out all the cords to her appliances, turns off the burners on the stove and switches off the overhead lights. The whole room goes black.)

No more cooking. I'm through!

CAL. *(Still on his knees, starts cleaning up the sauce with some towels.)* Ellen, what are you doing? There are people out there waiting for their food.

ELLEN. *(In a whisper.)* Too bad.

CAL. Half of them still haven't had their main course.

ELLEN. Go on, finish up the sauce on the floor. No one can see you.

CAL. Table one is still waiting for its entrees.

ELLEN. It's kind of nice like this . . .

CAL. Table Three may order second desserts . . .

ELLEN. . . . cozy . . .

CAL. Table Two can't make up its mind . . .

ELLEN. . . . comforting . . .

CAL. The next sitting will be here soon . . .

ELLEN. It's so quiet. *(She sits on one of the counters and hugs her legs to her chest.)*

CAL. A party of five is coming at nine.

ELLEN. Look at the stove Cal, it's moving.

CAL. We've got to keep ahead of them.

ELLEN. It's like some wonderful dark oceanliner . . .

CAL. ELLEN, LISTEN TO ME! All hell is going to break loose out there!

ELLEN. Cut free from its anchor . . .

CAL. I'm the one on the spot.

ELLEN. . . . pushing through the night . . .

CAL. What am I going to do?

ELLEN. No one can stop it.

CAL. (*In a panicy whisper.*) What am I going to do?

ELLEN. It's broken free and is heading out into places unknown.

SCENE 6

Lights up on DAVID OSSLOW *and* ELIZABETH BARROW COLT *who are waiting for their entrees.*

DAVID OSSLOW. Most publishing houses shy away from short story collections.

ELIZABETH BARROW COLT. (*Murmurs.*) Oh well, I didn't really . . .

DAVID OSSLOW. They just don't sell . . .

ELIZABETH BARROW COLT. (*Murmurs.*) Yes, I suppose when the chips are down . . .

DAVID OSSLOW. But yours are so remarkable. I'm sure people have told you that before.

ELIZABETH BARROW COLT. Actually, I don't see that many . . .

DAVID OSSLOW. I really appreciate you meeting me like this on such a cold . . .

ELIZABETH BARROW COLT. (*Giddy.*) I HAD NO

IDEA WHAT YOU LOOKED LIKE. I COULDN'T
IMAGINE HOW WE'D EVER . . .

CAL. (*Upset and rushed, plunges into the restaurant
and up to their table with the bass. Under his breath.*)
Please God, don't let them notice there's no Hollandaise
sauce on the bass . . . "Bar au Mousse de Crevettes"
(*He places it on the table with a flourish.*)

DAVID OSSLOW. Aaaahhhh, here comes our entree!

ELIZABETH BARROW COLT. Oh.

CAL. (*With very elaborate gestures.*) And would
you like me to divide it for you?

DAVID OSSLOW. Please.

CAL. (*Does a spectacular job preparing the fish.*)

DAVID OSSLOW. (*In a whisper as he works.*) Look
at that bass! It's a masterpiece!

(ELIZABETH BARROW COLT *peers at* CAL *nearsightedly,
then sneaks on her glasses to see better.*)

DAVID OSSLOW. I didn't know you wore glasses.

ELIZABETH BARROW COLT. (*Quickly takes them off.*)
Oh, I don't! These are someone else's.

DAVID OSSLOW. You wear someone else's glasses?

ELIZABETH BARROW COLT. Sylvia, Tussman, she
works downtown at Hyde and Johnson's . . .

DAVID OSSLOW. You could ruin your eyes wearing
someone else's glasses . . .

ELIZABETH BARROW COLT. . . . In the typing pool,
she's also good at steno.

DAVID OSSLOW. You should get your own prescrip-
tion.

ELIZABETH BARROW COLT. She has several different
pairs of glasses, so she said . . .

DAVID OSSLOW. (*Looking at her closely.*) You know,
you have very beautiful eyes.

ELIZABETH BARROW COLT. Oh no . . .

DAVID OSSLOW. You do. They're so pale, transparent almost . . .

ELIZABETH BARROW COLT. (*Blazing with embarrassment, drops her head, murmurs.*)

DAVID OSSLOW. (*Cups her face in his hands.*) Let me see them again . . .

ELIZABETH BARROW COLT. It's nothing, they're just . . . eyes . . .

DAVID OSSLOW. (*Drawing her head closer.*) No really, they're . . . extraordinary.

ELIZABETH BARROW COLT. I don't know, I . . .

DAVID OSSLOW. I bet they glow in the dark . . . They do, don't they?

ELIZABETH BARROW COLT. (*Has fallen in love with DAVID OSSLOW.*) Not really, I . . .

(CAL, *finished with his handiwork, tries to set* ELIZABETH'S *plate down, but she's all over the place. Just as he's about to put it down, she moves, blocking him. They play a dreadful kind of hesitation dance.*)

CAL. Sorry, I was just trying to . . . excuse me, I just wanted . . . *I'm sorry!* . . . Hold it right there . . . *if you could just steady her . . .*

ELIZABETH BARROW COLT. I'm sorry, I'm sorry, I'm sorry, I'm sorry, I'm sorry, I'm sorry . . .

DAVID OSSLOW. (*Holds her still with both hands.*)

CAL. (*Finally sets it down.*) There we are!

ELIZABETH BARROW COLT. (*Looks down at it.*) Gosh.

CAL. (*Sets down DAVID's plate with ease.*) And for Monsieur . . .

ELIZABETH BARROW COLT. (*Looking at her bass, unable to face DAVID OSSLOW.*) Gosh.

DAVID OSSLOW. (*Lifts his fork to her.*) Bon appetit! (*And dives in.*)

ELIZABETH BARROW COLT. (*Is paralyzed by shyness and can't move.*) Gosh . . . beautiful eyes!

DAVID OSSLOW. Are you all right?

ELIZABETH BARROW COLT. Oh dear.

DAVID OSSLOW. What's wrong?

ELIZABETH BARROW COLT. (*Starts to laugh breathlessly.*)

DAVID OSSLOW. Don't you like the bass?

ELIZABETH BARROW COLT. (*Trying to stop laughing.*) Oh dear, oh dear, oh dear.

DAVID OSSLOW. (*Laughs tentatively with her.*)

ELIZABETH BARROW COLT. (*Puts her napkin over her face in an effort to stop. Snorts and gasps under it.*) No one ever said I had beautiful . . .

DAVID OSSLOW. (*Watches her with amusement and then returns to his bass.*)

ELIZABETH BARROW COLT. (*Suddenly rises, pushes her chair back almost knocking it over, and with the napkin partially over her head, lurches towards the rear of the room.*)

DAVID OSSLOW. (*Stands.*) Are you all right?

CAL. The Ladies Room is to the left.

ELIZABETH BARROW COLT. (*Great peals of laughter erupting from her, careens into the kitchen.*)

CAL. She went into the kitchen . . .

DAVID OSSLOW. She's been wearing someone else's glasses.

CAL. Oh.

(ELIZABETH BARROW COLT *wanders nearsightedly through the dark kitchen, amazed at the confusion of food and pots.*)

DAVID OSSLOW. May we have our wine now please?
(*He keeps eating.*)

CAL. Certainly, sir.

DAVID OSSLOW. She's a writer.

CAL. Yes?

DAVID OSSLOW. And a very good one.

CAL. She looks like a writer.

DAVID OSSLOW. Mmmmm . . .

CAL. Strange eyes . . .

DAVID OSSLOW. I don't think she's been out to
restaurants very often.

ELIZABETH BARROW COLT. (*Bursts back into the
room, laughing.*) I was in the . . . kitchen . . . (*She
twirls around, confused, still looking for the Ladies'
Room . . . and following another route, ends up in
the kitchen again.*)

DAVID OSSLOW. (*Eating.*) This bass is delicious!

CAL. I'm so glad you like it! (*He puts down the
bottle of wine.*) Puligny-Montrachet.

DAVID OSSLOW. (*Nods that* CAL *should pour it, as
he continues to eat.*)

CAL. (*Uncorks the bottle and begins the ritual of
pouring it. He gives* DAVID *the cork to smell, pours him
a tiny taste, waits for his approval, fills* ELIZABETH'S
glass, and then returns to DAVID'S *as.*)

ELIZABETH BARROW COLT. (*Continues to wander
through the dark kitchen. She eventually comes upon*
ELLEN *who's sitting on the counter, peers nearsightedly
at her, and is unable to make any sense of what's happening. More embarrassed than ever, she lunges back
out into the restaurant.*) I was in the kitchen . . .
again . . . (*And helplessly tries to get her moorings.*)

CAL. Upstairs . . . the Ladies Room is *upstairs*
. . . to the left . . .

ELIZABETH BARROW COLT. (*Almost on all fours,
creeps out of the room.*)

CAL. *(As he watches her.)* Maybe she needs her glasses, she was wearing them earlier.

DAVID OSSLOW. No, I don't think so.

CAL. She seems lost . . .

DAVID OSSLOW. *(Drinking his wine.)* She'll be all right. *(A silence.)*

ELIZABETH BARROW COLT. *(Gingerly re-enters the room. She waves to David from afar.)* Oh dear. . .

DAVID OSSLOW. *(Rises, waves back.)* Hi.

ELIZABETH BARROW COLT. *(Softly.)* Hi.

DAVID OSSLOW. Are you feeling better? *(He pulls out her chair.)*

ELIZABETH BARROW COLT. *(She collapses into it.)* I'm sorry . . .

DAVID OSSLOW. Don't be sorry . . . *(He starts pushing her back to the table.)*

ELIZABETH BARROW COLT. I'm so embarrassed . . .

DAVID OSSLOW. Your bass is getting cold.

ELIZABETH BARROW COLT. *(Is overcome by embarrassment and starts to cry.)* I'm sorry . . .

CAL. Can I get you anything else?

DAVID OSSLOW. No, we're fine, thank you.

CAL. Then I'll be getting back to the kitchen. *(He rushes back to ELLEN, angry.)* ELLEN, PLEASE!

ELIZABETH BARROW COLT. Oh dear.

DAVID OSSLOW. *(Moving closer to her.)* Calm down.

ELIZABETH BARROW COLT. *(Can't stop crying.)* Oh dear, oh dear, oh dear . . .

DAVID OSSLOW. Elizabeth, it happens all the time.

ELIZABETH BARROW COLT. No.

DAVID OSSLOW. Yes. All the time. Now dry your eyes and eat your bass.

ELIZABETH BARROW COLT. *(Doesn't move.)* Yes.

DAVID OSSLOW. I've seen writers fall to the floor in

a dead faint.

ELIZABETH BARROW COLT. Oh.

DAVID OSSLOW. I've seen it all, believe me!

ELIZABETH BARROW COLT. (*Looks at her bass.*) Oh my . . .

DAVID OSSLOW. Now try some of that bass.

ELIZABETH BARROW COLT. Yes.

DAVID OSSLOW. It's supurb. You'll love it.

ELIZABETH BARROW COLT. (*Looks at her bass again, helpless. Sighs. A silence, then very loud and intense.*) ONE AFTERNOON WHEN I CAME HOME FROM SCHOOL MOTHER WAS IN TEARS BECAUSE LACEY HAD QUIT, WALKED OUT IN A TORRENT OF INSULTS. "NEVER AGAIN!", MOTHER SOBBED. "FROM NOW ON, I'LL DO THE COOKING MYSELF!" . . . IT WAS A BIG MISTAKE. SHE DIDN'T KNOW HOW AND SHE WAS IN THE MIDST OF MENOPAUSE. SHE KEPT BREAKING DISHES AND CUTTING HER FINGERS WITH THE CARVING KNIFE. ONE NIGHT SHE SLICED OFF THE TIP OF HER THUMB AND GROUND IT UP IN THE GARBAGE DISPOSAL!

(HANNAH GALT *lurches towards the Ladies' Room. The lights rise a little to reveal the other diners. They're startled by* ELIZABETH'S *sudden outburst and stare, then turn away feigning indifference, but hanging on every word.*)

ELIZABETH BARROW COLT. Mealtime was much the same as it had always been . . . Father still talked a blue streak, Mother still mashed her food into a pink soup. . . . and I still spit everything out into my napkin. But they were paper napkins now, and since I cleared the table, there was no chance of discovery. I breathed easier. What changed then, was the violence that went into the cooking beforehand . . . I never saw such blood letting over meals! If she didn't knick herself while cutting the tomatoes, she'd deliberately slice a finger while waiting for the rice to boil. "Why bother cooking?," she'd cry, holding her bleeding hands under the faucet. "We'll all be dead soon enough!" . . . It was around this time that Mother was starting to get . . . suicidal . . . (*She starts to laugh.*) Oh dear, I shouldn't laugh . . . it was just so . . . comical! You see, Mother was very comical. She wore hats all the time, great turban-type creations piled high with artificial flowers and paper maché fruits. She wore them outside and she wore them in the house. She wore them when she cooked and when she ate . . . great teetering crowns that bobbed and jingled with every move . . . poor Mother . . . I don't know what it was that made her so unhappy . . . her menopause, her cocktails before dinner, some private anguish . . . but during this period, she used to threaten to kill herself. After another blood stained dinner, she'd throw herself face down on our driveway and beg my father to put the car in reverse and drive over her. "Don't be ridiculous, dear," he'd say. But she meant it and would lie there sobbing, "PLEASE . . . DO IT!" It was a ritual we went through every night . . .

DAVID OSSLOW. (*Does his best to eat his dinner, stopping only when he's too shaken to swallow.*) And did she ever . . . ? I mean . . . succeed?

ELIZABETH BARROW COLT. (*Sighs.*) Oh dear.

DAVID OSSLOW. She did . . .

ELIZABETH BARROW COLT. Poor Mother.

DAVID OSSLOW. How . . . awful . . . ELIZABETH BARROW COLT. (*Sighs.*) Your father finally gave in and ran over her . . .

ELIZABETH BARROW COLT. Not that.

DAVID OSSLOW. Sleeping pills . . .

ELIZABETH BARROW COLT. If only it had been . . .

DAVID OSSLOW. Poor thing . . .

ELIZABETH BARROW COLT. Yes . . .

DAVID OSSLOW. She shot herself? . . .

ELIZABETH BARROW COLT. Can't you guess?

DAVID OSSLOW. How could I guess . . . with someone like . . . *that?*

ELIZABETH BARROW COLT. Think! It's so in character!

DAVID OSSLOW. She slit her throat with a carving knife?

ELIZABETH BARROW COLT. (*A bit blood thirsty.*) Better . . .

DAVID OSSLOW. (*After a pause.*) Of course . . . I know . . .

DAVID OSSLOW. She turned on the gas . . .	ELIZABETH BARROW COLT. She turned on the gas . . .

ELIZABETH BARROW COLT. She turned on the gas and opened that big mouth of an oven door and stuck her head in . . . with her hat firmly in place . . .

DAVID OSSLOW. Yes, of course . . . the hat!

ELIZABETH BARROW COLT. (*Starts laughing.*) It must have been quite a sight . . . mother down on all fours, trying to fit her head in without knocking her hat off . . .

DAVID OSSLOW. And . . . ?

ELIZABETH BARROW COLT. Oh dear, I shouldn't laugh . . .

DAVID OSSLOW. No, go on . . .

ELIZABETH BARROW COLT. Well, after she'd been in there for ten minutes or so, getting groggier and groggier, something went wrong. The paper maché trinkets on her hat began to sizzle and explode like little firecrackers. Within moments the entire hat was in flames.

She came to like a shot and raced to the sink . . . her head actually . . . *cooking!* She turned on the water full blast . . . her hat and all of her hair was consumed . . . but she survived. (*Pause.*) She joked about it afterwards . . . after the hospital stay and plastic surgery . . . about almost having barbecued herself like some amazing delicacy . . . some exotic . . . roast! "I BET I WOULD HAVE TASTED DAMNED GOOD!", she used to say, smacking her lips. (*Long pause.*) My mother is very beautiful, you know . . . she's so beautiful . . . people turn around.

HANNAH GALT. (*Re-enters the room and sits down. A silence.*)

DAVID OSSLOW. You haven't eaten any of your bass.

ELIZABETH BARROW COLT. (*Looking at it.*) Oh yes, my bass . . .

DAVID OSSLOW. (*With great tenderness.*) You haven't touched it.

ELIZABETH BARROW COLT. I'm sorry, I . . .

DAVID OSSLOW. (*Touching her cheek.*) It's getting cold . . .

ELIZABETH BARROW COLT. Yes, I guess it is . . .

DAVID OSSLOW. (*Dips her fork into her bass and holds it out to her like a father feeding his child.*) Come . . . just try it . . . one taste . . . (ELIZABETH BARROW COLT *looks at him helplessly, unable to take it. Neither of them move, and the lights fade around them.*)

SCENE 7

The kitchen. Everything is still in a blackout.

CAL. (*Softly.*) Ellen, I beg of you. Don't do this to me . . . to us!

SCENE 8

The lights rise on HERRICK SIMMONS, NESSA VOX *and*
  TONY STASSIO.)

HERRICK SIMMONS. (*In a whisper.*) The things you
overhear in restaurants . . .

NESSA VOX. (*Whistles her disbelief.*)

TONY STASSIO. I don't know . . .

HERRICK SIMMONS. Very strange . . .

NESSA VOX. (*Whistles again.*)

HERRICK SIMMONS. Poor thing . . .

NESSA VOX. She has such . . . beautiful eyes.
(*Silence.*)

HERRICK SIMMONS. Guess what happened to me
today?

TONY STASSIO. What?

HERRICK SIMMONS. (*Starts to laugh.*) You'll die!

NESSA VOX. Tell us!

HERRICK SIMMONS. I was . . . flashed.

TONY STASSIO. So . . . ?

HERRICK SIMMONS. By a . . . woman!

TONY STASSIO. Gee!

NESSA VOX. What did she flash?

HERRICK SIMMONS. A breast!

NESSA VOX. How wonderful!

TONY STASSIO. How sick!

HERRICK SIMMONS. It wasn't sick at all, it was really
quite beautiful. I mean, it was so unexpected. I'd just
had lunch with Phillip and was looking in Tiffany's
windows. I turned to cross 57th Street, and this very
pretty blond woman was crossing towards me. As we
passed each other, she smiled at me, lowered one side
of her blouse, and flashed a gleaming breast . . .

TONY STASSIO. Sick . . .

NESSA VOX. I love it!

TONY STASSIO. What did you do?

HERRICK SIMMONS. Nothing. I just looked at it.

TONY STASSIO. (*Starts sneaking tastes of her bass.*)
God! Did she say anything?

HERRICK SIMMONS. Not a word.

NESSA VOX. (*Also lighting into her veal.*) I love it!
Women finally getting up enough nerve to be flashers!

HERRICK SIMMONS. (*Starts gobbling her duck.*)

(*This sneaking of food begins as innocent picking,
    but gets uglier and uglier as their real hunger and
    shame sets in.*)

TONY STASSIO. But imagine . . . doing that . . .
showing your breast to a stranger . . .

NESSA VOX. What was it like?

TONY STASSIO. It's really kind of . . .

HERRICK SIMMONS. What was *what* like?

NESSA VOX. Her breast . . .

HERRICK SIMMONS. It was nice.

NESSA VOX. Was it round . . . or pendulous?

TONY STASSIO. (*Sneaks more bass.*)

HERRICK SIMMONS. Round.

NESSA VOX. (*Sneaks more veal.*) I think I'd die if I
had pendulous breasts! (*At times only one woman is
sneaking her food, at times they sneak in concert.*)

HERRICK SMITH. *Why?*

NESSA VOX. They're so . . . *ugly!*

TONY STASSIO. (*In a small voice.*) Mine are pendulous.

NESSA VOX. They are not!

TONY STASSIO. They are so!

HERRICK SIMMONS. (*To* TONY.) You have lovely
breasts!

TONY STASSIO. (*Softly.*) I have shitty breasts.

HERRICK SIMMONS. NO WOMAN HAS SHITTY
BREASTS!

NESSA VOX. Listen, mine are dappled.

HERRICK SIMMONS. I'M SORRY, BUT BREASTS ARE LIFE GIVING!

TONY STASSIO. Dappled?

NESSA VOX. (*Her head lowered.*) Spotted. You know how sometimes they get all . . .

HERRICK SIMMONS. I've never heard of spotted breasts!

NESSA VOX. Whenever I'm upset, they get . . . mottled.

HERRICK SIMMONS. Listen, alot of women . . .

TONY STASSIO. (*In a low voice.*) When I gain weight, mine get *really* pendulous! "Old bananas," my brother used to call me!

HERRICK SIMMONS. Alot of women are ashamed of their breasts, it's ridiculous!

NESSA VOX. There's some imbalance in my hormones.

TONY STASSIO. . . . in front of his friends.

HERRICK SIMMONS. They should be proud of them!

NESSA VOX. (*To* TONY.) At least you're not . . . spotted.

HERRICK SIMMONS. (*To* TONY.) One of mine is bigger than the other, but they're still terrific!

TONY STASSIO. I have trouble finding clothes that fit.

NESSA VOX. And don't think it isn't painful!

HERRICK SIMMONS. What the hell . . .

TONY STASSIO. It's a real problem.

NESSA VOX. It's not fair.

TONY STASSIO. Of course when I diet, they do deflate somewhat . . .

NESSA VOX. (*To* HERRICK.) How would you like a blotchy bosom?

HERRICK SIMMONS. I MEAN, WHAT CAN WE DO ABOUT IT? WHAT CAN WE POSSIBLY DO? (*The lights fade on their ravenous and unhappy faces as they openly plunge into their food.*)

SCENE 9

But they don't rise in the kitchen because ELLEN *is still sitting in the dark.* CAL *paces nervously. All is stillness for several moments.*

CAL. (*Turns on the speaker connected with the tape that plays in the restaurant. The third movement from J.S. Bach's Sonata No. 3 in E major for violin and harpsicord goes on.*) Ellen . . .

ELLEN. Oh, that's nice . . .

CAL. I can't even see you.

ELLEN. Nice to stop and rest . . .

CAL. Could I light a candle at least?

ELLEN. (*A long sigh.*)

CAL. (*Gets a candle and sets it into a head of lettuce or some other unlikely object and then lights it.*)

ELLEN. How pretty . . .

CAL. That's better. . .(*Silence.*) Remember when you used to prepare us dinner when we were first married? How I loved it! watching you cook in the dark...it was so romantic. I could hear your heart race as you tended your filets, stirred your sauces. . . I could never quite see what you were adding, rending, sauting. . .

ELLEN. You'd never get too close, but would watch from a distance, give me my room . . . and all the time in the world. So much time and so much love . . .

CAL. Yes, I could feel it thickening all around us. I'd sneak glances at you in the darkness and reel at your grace . . . We were so happy! My God! That newly-wed cooking, those honeymoon suppers that lasted and lasted . . .

ELLEN. And here we are again except now you've eaten everything before I could get started . . . *why Cal?*

CAL. Because it's so good.

ELLEN. But it's *not* good! You're eating everything before it's done!

CAL. You're such a good cook . . .

ELLEN. You're eating it raw!

CAL. You have such a gift . . .

ELLEN. . . . gobbling it up . . .

CAL. . . . an incredible gift!

ELLEN. . . . swallowing it whole!

CAL. It's wonderful.

ELLEN. I can't go on like this.

CAL. Really . . . wonderful!

ELLEN. You've got to give me a chance . . . LET ME DO MY WORK! PLEASE . . . ! (*A silence.*)

CAL. (*Starts eating a roll.*) It's this damned not sleeping. I lie awake half the night worrying.

ELLEN. Just let me cook!

CAL. Will we pay off the loan?

ELLEN. I'll go sour without it, you know, soft at the edges, dead at the core!

CAL. . . . bring in some cash?

ELLEN. I don't care about cash!

CAL. Worrying makes me hungry, you know. Not sleeping makes me hungry.

ELLEN. I can't stop cooking, I've been at it too long

CAL. It all adds up.

ELLEN. You can still make a choice.

CAL. I know it's a problem.

ELLEN. And you must . . . or we're done for. Totally done for. (*A silence*)

CAL. I'll try and watch it.

ELLEN. You have to watch it.

CAL. And if for some terrible reason I can't?

ELLEN. It's over.

CAL. The restaurant will close?

ELLEN. No. everything's over. Finished *(A silence.)*

CAL. Even me?

ELLEN. *(Looks at him takes her time.)* Even you...

CAL. Ellen, don't say that.

ELLEN. It's true.

CAL. I said, *don't!* You don't help matters, you know..."Taste this...try that...Is it good? Oh Cal, will they like it?...I want them to die over it"...There's no escaping you and your outstretched spoon, did you ever think about that?

ELLEN. I was just asking you to taste, not eat the ground out from under me.

CAL. I know, I know.

ELLEN. You're out of control.

CAL. I know. *(Silence)*

ELLEN. Well then, here we sit.

CAL. *(In a whisper)* But there are hungry people out there.

ELLEN. So...?

CAL. Two of the tables are still waiting for their desserts.

ELLEN. So...?

CAL. The next group will be coming soon. *(Ellen sighs contentedly)*

CAL. This is starting to get scarey.

ELLEN. Gee, I'm beginning to enjoy it.

CAL. Can I turn on the light, at least?

ELLEN. Whatever you want.

CAL. *(Does)* Now I can see you, anyway. *(Ellen smiles and waves at him)*

CAL. *(Holds out a large wooden spoon to her)* Come on, baby...*(She won't take it)*

CAL. Please? *(He tries presenting it to her in a variety of coy ways: hiding it behind his back, trying to press it into her arms like a bouquet of flowers, pressing it up against her cheek, handling it like a baton, a flute, a sword)* Ellen. . .Ellen! Come on, cook!

ELLEN. Why?

CAL. For us, honey. . .for us! *(He tries more ploys with the spoon)*

ELLEN. I'm just too tired.

CAL. OK, OK, you want me to change. I'll change. . . WATCH THIS! *(He rushes over to the stove and with great bravura begins melting some butter in a skillet)*

ELLEN. Cal, what are you doing?

CAL. *(Performs these actions as he describes them)* He melts the butter in the pan with nary a lick. . .then he grates a soupçon of orange rind into the butter without touching his fingers to his lips. . .

ELLEN. *(Starts to laugh)* Cal. . .

CAL. *(More and more florrid)* Next, he adds a hint of maraschino and a dash of Curacao. . .Note how he inhales the fragrance of the mixture without taking a taste. . .

ELLEN. You forgot the sugar.

CAL. In a phenomenal display of speed and grace, he manages to add four tablespoons of sugar before the sauce comes to a boil. . .And once again, I'd like to draw your attention to the fact that never once does the aromatic spoon approach his lips. . .

ELLEN. Honey, you don't know how to make orange sauce.

CAL. *(Blends the ingredients, adding subtle hints of port and cassis. . .)*

ELLEN. Not cassis, Cal. . .kirsch!

CAL. *(Correcting his error)* Of course, of course, how stupid of me. . .*(He stirs and inhales with rising intensity)* Please note how he adjusts the flavoring through smell and not taste — how he relies exclusively on the prowess of his olfactory glands. . .

ELLEN. *(Goes to him and puts her arms around him)* Oh, Cal. . .

CAL. Ah ah, not too close. We don't want anything to

spill.

ELLEN. Cal. . . !

CAL. *(Then in one fluid move, he pours the sauce into an appropriate serving bowl)* And now to find something that looks like Crepes Suzettes. . . *(He roots around in the refrigerator and pulls out a stack of pancakes.)* Ahh, here we go. . . the Swedish pancakes you prepared for a rainy day. . . *(He puts them in the oven for a moment and kisses Ellen on the cheek)* You're really amazing you know. *(He turns the heat way up.)*

ELLEN. Cal, what *are* you doing?

CAL. Oh, the power of invention. . . ! *(He launches into an exuberant dance while singing an aria to the pancakes. He then removes them from the oven and puts them on a tray along with the sauce.)*

ELLEN. *(Laughing)* What's going on here?

CAL. It's my treat, my offering to the evening. *(He hands her the tray.)*

ELLEN. Wait a minute, why are you giving this to me?

CAL. Because you're going to bring it out when I give you the signal.

ELLEN. But I can't go out there.

CAL. Oh yes you can. We're in this together.

ELLEN. *(Protesting)* Cal. . . !

CAL. *(Plunks the tray into her arms and straightens out her apron, maybe even adding her chef's hat)* It's a beginning, Ellen. A beginning.

ELLEN. *(Teetering under the weight of the tray, laughing)* You're crazy, you know that?. . . Stark, raving. . .

CAL. And you. . . ? What about you?
(Ellen looks at him out of brimming eyes as he glides into the dining room.)

Scene 10

*The lights rise on the diners who are in considerable
agitation.*

DAVID OSSLOW. Waiter, could we see the dessert
menu, please?

HANNAH. *There* he is!

NESSA VOX. (*Hailing him.*) Sir?

PAUL. Well, finally! I thought he'd died in there!

NESSA VOX. *Sir??*

CAL. *(Fussing with a chafing dish.)* O.K., Ellen, wait 'til
the count of three.)

HANNAH. (*To* PAUL.) Ask him if they take Master
Charge?

DAVID OSSLOW. Waiter?

NESSA VOX. Excuse me, Sir. Could you possibly turn
up the heat a little more? It's freezing in here!

CAL. One...

TONY STASSIO. (*Rising to get her coat.*) I'm getting
my coat. It must be 90 below out there.

NESSA VOX. (*Also rises, stands by the window.*) Get
mine too . . .

PAUL. Waiter, the check please!

CAL. Two...

DAVID OSSLOW. Anytime you're ready with the dessert menu . . .

HANNAH. (*To* CAL.) Excuse me, but do you take
Master Charge?

DAVID OSSLOW. We'd also like a look at the pastry
tray.

PAUL. Waiter?! It's been half an hour!

CAL. Three!

ELLEN. (*Steps into the restaurant and puts the sauce and pancakes down on the chafing dish.*)

TONY STASSIO. What's happening?

HANNAH. What's this?

NESSA VOX. Who's that?

PAUL. What's going on?

TONY STASSIO. Who's she?

DAVID OSSLOW. It must be their dessert . . .

HERRICK SIMMONS. (*Returning from the Ladies' Room.*) It must be my zabaglione . . .

HANNAH. But we've already . . .

PAUL. Sssssshhhhhh!

HANNAH. Oh Paul, smell!

HERRICK SIMMONS. I love it!

ELLEN. (*To* CAL.) The matches please.

CAL. (*Lights a match to the dessert. Orange and blue flames leap up.*)

HANNAH. (*Gasps.*)

PAUL. Hannah hold still!

NESSA VOX. It looks like . . .

DAVID OSSLOW. It must be . . .

HANNAH. Oh, what's that called . . . ?

NESSA VOX. I've got it! (*A pause.*)

NESSA, DAVID, and HANNAH. It's Crepes Suzettes!

HANNAH. Crepes Suzettes!

HERRICK SIMMONS. Crepes Suzettes!

PAUL. I knew it!

CAL. (*Stands back and announces.*) CREPES CARROUSELS!

EVERYONE. (*Bursts into applause and sighs, murmurs of "Crepes Carrousels!"*)

CAL. . . . On the house!

EVERYONE. (*Even louder cheers and echoes of "On the house!"*)

ELLEN. (*Starts transferring the crepes into a large serving platter.*)

TONY STASSIO. I don't believe this!

HERRICK SIMMONS. (*Sidles over to the platter and looks in.*)

ELLEN. (*Motions her to help herself.*)

HERRICK SIMMONS. (*She does and sits back down at her place, smiling.*)

DAVID OSSLOW. (*Advances to take his piece.*) I've been to *many* restaurants in my day, but this is the first time I've ever seen anything like this!

NESSA VOX. Wait for me! (*She rushes to the platter and takes her share.*)

TONY STASSIO. I'm right behind you!

HANNAH. (*Helping herself.*) This is extraordinary.

ELIZABETH BARROW COLT. No, not really.

EVERYONE. (*Looks at her, suddenly hushed.*)

ELIZABETH BARROW COLT. It's like the beginning of time . . .

NESSA VOX and TONY STASSIO. (*Start to laugh.*)

DAVID OSSLOW. Ssssshhhhh!

HERRICK SIMMONS. Be quiet!

ELIZABETH BARROW COLT. *(With great simplicity.)* . . . long, long ago when men ate by a fire . . . crouched close to its warmth . . . entwined their great arms . . . gave thanks for the kill . . . and shared in the feast! *(She rises and joins the other diners at the flaming platter. She helps herself to some crepes and for the first time all evening, she eats. She looks at Ellen who smiles at her.)*

(*The diners become more jovial around* ELLEN *and eat with increased gusto, wiping their greasy faces, grunting with pleasure.* ELLEN *throws* CAL *a backward glance, but he shakes his head indicating he's eaten enough for the evening.* EVERYONE's *movements slow down to simple gestures, their language becomes less familiar. The fury of the November*

wind increases outside and the light from ELLEN'S
*bonfire burns brighter and brighter as the diners
gather close to its warmth.* ELLEN *stands above
them, churning up the flames, her face glowing
with a fierce radiance. Purified of their collective
civilization and private grief, they feast as* . . .)

THE CURTAIN SLOWLY FALLS

PROPERTY LIST—Author's note

Since the first edition was burdened with a 24 page prop list based on the New York Shakespeare Festival/ Kennedy Center production, this seems the perfect opportunity to replace excess with common sense. The play doesn't need 24 pages of props and groceries! I've heard of productions that managed with budgets of a few hundred dollars, I also know of a staging that used no food at all! The actors simply mimed its abundance, feasting on thin air. An extreme approach perhaps, certainly a brave one.

The key to any successful production has to do with using the resources at hand. If you're a penniless theater bursting with imagination, then use cookies and jello and...*pretend!* If you have a workable budget and live in a community with a fairly good gourmet restaurant, then press it into service for help and inspiration. In fact, this is exactly what most theaters do — link up with their local chefs for cooking lessons and short cuts. It's free publicity for the restaurant and instant celebrity for the chef who suddenly has this captive audience of actors and crew. For the company, it's an initiation into a whole new art form. The limits of collaboration are endless. I heard of one production in upper New York state in which the consulting restaurant got so carried away, it served the entire audience crepes suzettes on closing night. The trap of course, is letting the food swamp the performances. Finally it's crucial to remember the play is about appetite. It's what the food *represents* that makes it mouth-watering, not its myriad ingredients.

TONY STASSIO
raspberry dress
plum print jacket
raspberry sequined cap
pair raspberry sandals
black and raspberry bangle bracelet
triple strand raspberry beads
pair raspberry big button earrings
raspberry velvet bag

HERRICK SIMMONS
copper dress
copper half slip
2 pair textured pantyhose
7 graduated-length necklaces (gold chains)
5 gold rings
glass cameo pin
gold stick pin
gold initial "H" pin
gold bangle bracelet
pair gold big button earrings
pair beige sandals
tan "alligator" bag

ELIZABETH BARROW COLT
2 grey and maroon print dresses
3 brown full slips
3 pair underpants
brown print knit tam
pair matching gloves
pair natural leather sandals

HANNAH GALT
maroon silk dress
2 black half slips
strand pearls
triple strand necklace (1 pearl; 2 chain)
beaded bangle bracelet
pair black suede pumps
black silk bag

ELLEN
blue flowered cotton dress
2 white aprons

blue denim apron
2 large white chefs hats
small white chefs hat
red plaid flannel shirt
pair beige espadrilles

PAUL GALT
3 piece grey suit
2 pair black socks with grey stripe at top
2 blue shirts with white collar
grey silk tie
pair black shoes
tan wallet
"Queen Mary" stick pin
2 pearl tie tacks
2 gold tie bars
2 gold collar pins
blue and grey silk handkerchief
set grey suspenders

DAVID OSSLOW
pair brown flannel trousers
2 tan plaid shirts
brown knit tie
brown tweed jacket with elbow patches
2 pair green argyle socks
pair brown shoes
brown 1½" belt

CAL
pair black tuxedo trousers
black tuxedo jacket
5 white formal shirts
black bow tie
2 pair red knit socks
pair red nylon socks
2 pair black socks
2 pair gold cuff links
pair black cuff links
silver pocket watch
2 pair shoelaces

COSTUME PLOT

COATS
WOMEN
  black mink
  dusty rose wool
  brown velvet
  tan lined trenchcoat
MEN
  camel cashmere with paisley scarf and gloves

Other Publications for Your Interest

A WEEKEND NEAR MADISON
(LITTLE THEATRE—COMIC DRAMA)
By KATHLEEN TOLAN

2 men, 3 women—Interior

This recent hit from the famed Actors Theatre of Louisville, a terrific ensemble play about male-female relationships in the 80's, was praised by *Newsweek* as "warm, vital, glowing . . . full of wise ironies and unsentimental hopes". The story concerns a weekend reunion of old college friends now in their early thirties. The occasion is the visit of Vanessa, the queen bee of the group, who is now the leader of a lesbian/feminist rock band. Vanessa arrives at the home of an old friend who is now a psychiatrist hand in hand with her naif-like lover, who also plays in the band. Also on hand are the psychiatrist's wife, a novelist suffering from writer's block; and his brother, who was once Vanessa's lover and who still loves her. In the course of the weekend, Vanessa reveals that she and her lover desperately want to have a child—and she tries to persuade her former male lover to father it, not understanding that he might have some feelings about the whole thing. *Time Magazine* heard "the unmistakable cry of an infant hit . . . Playwright Tolan's work radiates promise and achievement." (#25051)

(Royalty, $60–$40.)

PASTORALE
(LITTLE THEATRE—COMEDY)
By DEBORAH EISENBERG

3 men, 4 women—Interior
(plus 1 or 2 bit parts and 3 optional extras)

"Deborah Eisenberg is one of the freshest and funniest voices in some seasons."—Newsweek. Somewhere out in the country Melanie has rented a house and in the living room she, her friend Rachel who came for a weekend but forgets to leave, and their school friend Steve (all in their mid-20s) spend nearly a year meandering through a mental landscape including such concerns as phobias, friendship, work, sex, slovenliness and epistemology. Other people happen by: Steve's young girlfriend Celia, the virtuous and annoying Edie, a man who Melanie has picked up in a bar, and a couple who appear during an intense conversation and observe the sofa is on fire. The lives of the three friends inevitably proceed and eventually draw them, the better prepared perhaps by their months on the sofa, in separate directions. "The most original, funniest new comic voice to be heard in New York theater since Beth Henley's 'Crimes of the Heart.'"—N.Y. Times. "A very funny, stylish comedy."—The New Yorker. "Wacky charm and wayward wit."—New York Magazine. "Delightful."—N.Y. Post. "Uproarious . . . the play is a world unto itself, and it spins."—N.Y. Sunday Times. (#18016)

(Royalty, $50–$35.)

Other Publications for Your Interest

TALKING WITH...
(LITTLE THEATRE)
By JANE MARTIN

11 women—Bare stage

Here, at last, is the collection of eleven extraordinary monologues for eleven actresses which had them on their feet cheering at the famed Actors Theatre of Louisville—audiences, critics and, yes, even jaded theatre professionals. The mysteriously pseudonymous Jane Martin is truly a "find", a new writer with a wonderfully idiosyncratic style, whose characters alternately amuse, move and frighten us always, however, speaking to us from the depths of their souls. The characters include a baton twirler who has found God through twirling; a fundamentalist snake handler, an ex-rodeo rider crowded out of the life she has cherished by men in 3-piece suits who want her to dress up "like Minnie damn Mouse in a tutu"; an actress willing to go to any length to get a job; and an old woman who claims she once saw a man with "cerebral walrus" walk into a McDonald's and be healed by a Big Mac. "Eleven female monologues, of which half a dozen verge on brilliance."—London Guardian. "Whoever (Jane Martin) is, she's a writer with an original imagination."—Village Voice. "With Jane Martin, the monologue has taken on a new poetic form, intensive in its method and revelatory in its impact."—Philadelphia Inquirer. "A dramatist with an original voice . . . (these are) tales about enthusiasms that become obsessions, eccentric confessionals that levitate with religious symbolism and gladsome humor."—N.Y. Times. *Talking With . . .* is the 1982 winner of the American Theatre Critics Association Award for Best Regional Play.   (#22009)

(Royalty, $60–$40.
If individual monologues are done separately: Royalty, $15–$10.)

HAROLD AND MAUDE
(ADVANCED GROUPS—COMEDY)
By COLIN HIGGINS

9 men, 8 women—Various settings

Yes: *the Harold and Maude!* This is a stage adaptation of the wonderful movie about the suicidal 19 year-old boy who finally learns how to truly *live* when he meets up with that delightfully whacky octogenarian, Maude. Harold is the proverbial Poor Little Rich Kid. His alienation has caused him to attempt suicide several times, though these attempts are more cries for attention than actual attempts. His peculiar attachment to Maude, whom he meets at a funeral (a mutual passion), is what saves him—and what captivates us. This new stage version, a hit in France directed by the internationally-renowned Jean-Louis Barrault, will certainly delight both afficionados of the film and new-comers to the story. "Offbeat upbeat comedy."—Christian Science Monitor.   (#10032)

(Royalty, $60–$40.)

Other Publications for Your Interest

THE CURATE SHAKESPEARE
AS YOU LIKE IT
(LITTLE THEATRE—COMEDY)

By DON NIGRO

4 men, 3 women—Bare stage

This extremely unusual and original piece is subtitled: "The record of one company's attempt to perform the play by William Shakespeare". When the very prolific Mr. Nigro was asked by a professional theatre company to adapt *As You Like It* so that it could be performed by a company of seven he, of course, came up with a completely original play about a rag-tag group of players comprised of only seven actors led by a dotty old curate who nonetheless must present Shakespeare's play; and the dramatic interest, as well as the comedy, is in their hilarious attempts to impersonate all of Shakespeare's multitude of characters. The play has had numerous productions nationwide, all of which have come about through word of mouth. We are very pleased to make this "underground comic classic" widely available to theatre groups who like their comedy wide open and theatrical.   (#5742)

(Royalty, $50-$25.)

SEASCAPE WITH SHARKS
AND DANCER
(LITTLE THEATRE—DRAMA)

By DON NIGRO

1 man, 1 woman—Interior

This is a fine new play by an author of great talent and promise. We are very glad to be introducing Mr. Nigro's work to a wide audience with *Seascape With Sharks and Dancer*, which comes directly from a sold-out, critically acclaimed production at the world-famous Oregon Shakespeare Festival. The play is set in a beach bungalow. The young man who lives there has pulled a lost young woman from the ocean. Soon, she finds herself trapped in his life and torn between her need to come to rest somewhere and her certainty that all human relationships turn eventually into nightmares. The struggle between his tolerant and gently ironic approach to life and her strategy of suspicion and attack becomes a kind of war about love and creation which neither can afford to lose. In other words, this is quite an offbeat, wonderful love story. We would like to point out that the play also contains a wealth of excellent *monologue* and *scene material.*   (#21060)

(Royalty, $50-$35.)